"Do You Still Ask Pin a Lot of Things, Leon?"

"Why?"

"I just wondered. I heard the doctor and mother talking about you and Pin. They don't like the way you talk about him all the time. . . I don't think we'll be able to talk about Pin in front of them anymore, Leon."

"You're probably right."

"We'll keep him to ourselves, huh?" There was some new excitement in her eyes. She walked over and sat on my bed. "I mean, we won't ever mention his name in front of them anymore, OK?"

"I suppose so."

"I think Pin is a very lonely person," she said. Her tone of voice indicated she wanted to play one of those create-your-own-world games. I wasn't in the mood, and besides, Pin wasn't a toy. "I think he wishes he could live here with us. What do you think?"

"Yes," I said. "I think he does."

"Miriam Cohen isn't half as pretty as I am, is she, Leon? Not half as pretty." She looked at herself in my dresser mirror and stroked her hair. I thought about what she had said about keeping Pin a secret. The idea made my heart beat faster. I was afraid, afraid of . . . losing him.

ANDREW NEIDERMAN

PIN

PUBLISHED BY POCKET BOOKS NEW YORK

Another *Original* publication of POCKET BOOKS

POCKET BOOKS, a Simon & Schuster division of
GULF & WESTERN CORPORATION
1230 Avenue of the Americas, New York, N.Y. 10020

ISBN: 0-671-41501-8

First Pocket Books printing April, 1981

10 9 8 7 6 5 4 3 2 1

POCKET and colophon are trademarks of Simon & Schuster.

Printed in the U.S.A.

For my sister, "Zane",
who hears the same voices.

Acknowledgment

Heartfelt thanks to Anita Diamant and Humphrey Evans III for their faith. Gratitude, appreciation and respect to Ann Patty, a creative editor, a literary jewel.

PIN

PROLOGUE

WE ARE HYPNOTIZED BY THE SILENCE, ESPECIALLY ON winter nights when there are no stars and the streetlights wash the skeleton-white snow in a sickly pale yellow. Beyond the reach of the streetlights, there is a deep blackness that soaks into my memory. I struggle to pull shapes and sounds out of the past, but I have little success. I know that the bodies and the voices are there. They torment me. Sometimes I hear a word or catch the glimpse of a familiar face. But in an instant, they are gone.

I have the same dream every night. I'm asleep and I feel soft fingertips tracing the lines of my mouth, moving slowly up my cheeks and pressing softly on my eyes. I try desperately to open them, but I am unable to do it. I want to shout, but my lips won't

2

part. Finally I settle for hoping I can cry so a tear can escape my clamped eyelids, but even that never happens.

Sometimes during the daytime, she will wheel me before a mirror and leave me there to stare at myself for hours. She even does it at night if the whim comes into her head. I don't know what she expects this will do. I know she enjoys doing it. She laughs and says, "There." She'll stand behind me and look at both of us in the mirror. Sometimes she's naked and presses her breasts against my head. I see them there and know that I should feel them and wonder why I don't. It makes me think I'm watching two other people, that I'm looking through a window instead of into a mirror.

There are times when I can hear the music she plays. It's mostly music that we both enjoy. At times she will play music she's not really fond of, but music she knows I enjoy. I know that I like the music; I remember that it gave me pleasure to listen to it, but I don't have the same feelings now. I wonder about that, but I don't try to understand any changes in myself.

I suppose I don't think very much, or at least not in the way most people think. I hear her words and see her move about, but I don't react. I know when she's laughing; I know when she's crying. I sense when she is angry. She is always reciting names at me. Sometimes, she shouts them. I know they are names, but I can't relate them to any faces. This enrages her and she storms about.

There are times when she will sit quietly with me and not say a word for hours. It's like we're both waiting for something or maybe someone. It could very well be we're waiting for someone to come

home. I don't know. I try to remember who it could be we're waiting for, but I am unable to think of anyone. When she grows tired of this, she will get up, pace about a bit, and then sigh and leave the room.

I never mind the silence. When there is a complete silence, I feel encased in it. It brings a warmth I would otherwise not have. Recently, however, I was terribly bothered by the sound of my own heartbeat. The thumping reverberated through every bone in my body, especially the bones of my skull. It began as a minor annoyance and then grew to be terrible. The first time it happened, it lasted for a short while. Then it lasted longer and longer. Yesterday, it lasted nearly all day.

Of course I can't control it. If I hold my breath, it just beats faster. I know what's happening: parts of my body are revolting, going off on their own. I am literally falling apart. Someone else would panic, but I have always remained calm, steadfast in any crisis.

She knows something is wrong. She looks at me differently.

"You're flushed," she says. "I haven't seen you flushed for a long time. Maybe you're having a sexual thought. Are you having a sexual thought?"

She feels my forehead. I know she's feeling it because she's standing right before me and her hand is extended down toward me and out of sight. I don't feel her hand. I want to feel her hand; I even long to feel her hand, but it is as though she has no hand or I have no head.

"Oh God," she says, "you're ice cold as usual." She steps back and looks at me. "There's ice in your eyes."

She sits across from me and stares at me for the longest time. Her face has little expression. I think she's trying to reflect what she sees in me.

"When I die," she says, "I hope I die in this chair staring at you and I hope you stare at me until you die."

There is no hate in her voice. I remember the sound of hate and I would recognize it if I heard it. Her statement is more like a statement of fact. It's a good statement and I feel myself almost considering it. But it dies quickly, disappearing like a streak of lightning, singeing the blackness in my mind.

It works like an incision, though, and some thoughts seep through the darkness, oozing down to the threshold of where they could become words if I could still make words. I hear them clearly in my own mind and for a few moments I am terribly excited. I am like a man in solitary confinement for a lifetime finally hearing another human voice.

I look at her and I think:

"We were not always alone like this, you and I. There was someone else here sharing our solitude."

If she could hear me, she would say, "Yes, yes. Go on."

"I'm not talking about our mother and our father."

"No, no."

"But it's someone who was with us for nearly our whole lives."

"Yes."

"I can't . . . see his face, but I can hear his voice. I know this voice."

"Go on, go on."

"He's calling, calling."

She's so happy; she's so excited. She knows I'm going to pull him out of the darkness. He's within my reach. I can feel his hand. It's as cold as mine, but I do not let go. I pull harder and harder until he is brought back. Then I see his face.

"It's Pin," I say. "Pin, Pin."

As soon as I am able to say it, it all begins again.

Chapter 1

I WAS SITTING BY THE WINDOW LOOKING OUT AT THE heavy snowfall and trying to follow the descent of just one flake at a time, just to see if I could do it. I couldn't because the flakes kept whirling away in the wind. Pin sat back in his corner of the room and watched me. Although I didn't turn around, I knew he was smirking the same way my father used to smirk whenever he thought I was doing something silly. Every once in a while, Pin would say, "Well, well?" in that same high nasal pitch my father used when he spoke to us or to other children through Pin. It was very annoying, but I ignored him for as long as I could. Finally, frustrated, I turned around.

"I can't do it," I said. There was no longer a smirk

8

on Pin's face. His eyes glared with my father's arrogance.

"Did you really expect you could?" I could see he was satisfied. He loved being right. I remembered one time when I was with my father in the hospital corridor and he was telling this tiny, elderly woman that her husband was in the throes of a heart attack. She asked, "Are you sure? Are you sure? Maybe it's just a chest cold." She looked from him to me as though I could support her hope. I looked up at my father. He hated to be contradicted, especially by a patient or relatives of a patient. He would go into a rage if nurses ever did it. His eyes became small and intense, just the way Pin's were now, and his jawbone tightened so hard the little nerves in the sides of his cheeks quivered and twitched. Because anyone could see right through Pin's face, it was easy to know when he was upset.

"Your husband, madam, is having a coronary. I would estimate that seventy percent of his heart muscle has been destroyed. Pretending it's something else will not make it go away. I suggest you remain in the waiting room and call some of your closest relatives." With that he walked away. I practically had to run to keep up with him. When I looked back at the little woman, I saw she was still standing there, holding her hands against her chest.

"The idea of someone trying to follow one snowflake," Pin said. He gave the equivalent of what had always been my father's laugh: a short, guttural sound centered in the throat. I was really very disgusted with him and almost left him sitting there in the room alone. I've done that before. He's always pretended that it doesn't bother him. "Your

9

father never minded solitude, why should I?" he said. But I know it bothers him because he told Ursula that it did and she told me. That was a long time ago when she was just a little girl.

When we were young, each of us made out that he'd keep the strictest confidence about anything Pin said, but we didn't. I used to tell her everything and she used to tell me everything. Now she rarely says anything about her conversations with Pin. Actually, I don't think she talks to him much. At least, that's the impression I get. I know she has developed this thing about dressing him and absolutely refuses to help keep him clean. It's so important that he be kept clean. My father always made a point of that. Through Pin he would say, "Cleanliness is the foundation for good health." And then when little kids would come into the office, he would have Pin say, "Do you wash your face and hands regularly and especially before eating? I do." The kids would laugh and then look at my father, but his lips were tightly closed and he would always act as though he was interested in something else and had nothing to do with Pin's voice.

"Your father oughta be in show business," people often told me and Ursula, but I didn't think so. He wasn't interested in performing for anyone but himself.

"Did you really think you had the visual discrimination to follow one snowflake in this blizzard?" Pin said, pronouncing each word deliberately, just to ridicule my idea.

"No," I said. "Damnit."

"No reason to get emotional, Leon. You're getting more and more high strung lately, jumping at everything I say; and you snap at Ursula before she

completes a sentence, just like your father used to do to people. It's not at all like you. Maybe you should pop a pill, hmm?"

"Maybe you should shut up for a minute."

"See what I mean?"

He was exasperating sometimes, sitting there in that wheelchair, bulldozing and manipulating me. I felt like going over to him, twisting off the top of his skull, and reaching in to pinch his rippled, rubbery brain. I've looked at it up close a number of times. He's really amazing, every part of him. The brain even has the tiny veins running through it. You can see how all the nerve endings are attached and how the eyes are connected. He doesn't like me doing that anymore—looking into him like that—and I haven't really done it since my parents died.

I turned my back on him and looked out the window again. Mr. Machinsky was trying to make a broken U-turn on the snowy street, and traffic was blocked up as far as I could see down the hill. They were all skiers, impatient to get up to Davos, the ski resort built at the top of the mountain. They started leaning on their horns. This made old Machinsky nervous and he pounded on his horn, rather than continuing his turn. It seemed to work. They all shut up and waited. Some leaned out of their windows and yelled at him as he drove down the road, but the old man ignored them. He was tough and stubborn and the only neighbor we had at this point on the hill. I always kept away from his property because I knew he hated kids and my mother had said, "Machinsky is so dirty he's a host for all sorts of germs. I wouldn't want to ever rub up against him." She had actually shivered and embraced herself, squeezing her small but shapely breasts against each

— 11

other. She wore her dark brown hair tied back in a bun because "it was the neatest and cleanest way to keep it." Although she had a fine wardrobe, she mainly wore housecoats starched as clean as surgical gowns. I used to think that those tiny veins in her temples and on the tops of her hands were so visible because she scrubbed herself so vigorously. I remember asking my father about it.

"Ridiculous," he said without looking at me. He was reading one of his medical journals. "Her hygienic habits have nothing to do with her skin density."

"Are Pin's veins as close to the surface as anyone else's?"

He put his magazine aside and looked at me as though he had just realized I was actually there.

"Everything about Pin—his dimensions, his organs, even the irises in his eyes, everything—is representative. For his body size, that is." He snapped his magazine before him again and I was quiet.

My father wasn't a large man, although his demeanor and his appearance always made him seem bigger than he was. People were genuinely surprised when they learned that he was barely five feet ten inches tall and weighed one hundred and sixty pounds. He wore his thin black hair cut short, like a marine drill instructor, and he shaved twice a day because his beard was so dark and heavy. I was always in awe of his hands, with their long, powerful fingers. Anyone who ever had it done said he could put stitches in so quickly it was practically a painless experience.

Mr. Machinsky's self-made traffic jam had been

amusing, so I laughed. Pin was dying to ask me why I was laughing, but he didn't. I knew he was keeping silent just for spite, so I didn't say anything. I wasn't really that talkative a person anyway. I suppose I inherited that from my father, who was always disdainful of small talk. He didn't have the tolerance for it. My mother was forever too busy for idle chatter. She worked at the house with a nervous energy that consumed her every waking moment. It is a big house and although we could easily afford live-in servants, my mother insisted she had to do it all herself. If a maid cleaned up anything, she'd only go in after her, dissatisfied with the job. My father was by no means frugal, but he made no effort to get her any domestic help. If I asked him any questions about my mother, as I did about her veins, he would sluff it off when at home. If I asked him questions about my mother or about Ursula or even myself when he was at the office, he would answer through Pin. In fact, when I give it some deep thought, I realize he would very rarely speak directly to me. I know we never had what other guys would call a down-to-earth father-son discussion. He often gave me the feeling he resented me. I think he thought of me as his "offspring" rather than his son.

When my father was in a halfway decent mood at the office, and there were no patients, he would let Pin give me a lecture on something medical. I would pull my little chair up in front of Pin and my father would stand off behind me, cleaning instruments or something, and suddenly Pin would speak with my father's high-pitched nasal voice. In the beginning, I would turn around to ask a question, but after a while, I would just ask Pin the questions. Sometimes

Ursula was there and would do the same, but she
didn't have the same patience or interest and often
grew bored.

As long as I can remember, both Ursula and I
called him "doctor." I think that stemmed from my
mother always referring to him that way. "You'd
better get your things together before the doctor
comes home." "Tell the doctor his supper's ready."
So we called him "doctor" instead of dad or pop. Of
course, Pin never referred to him directly as anything but "the doctor."

Bored with the falling snow and the continuous
traffic of skiers, I turned away from the window
again just as Ursula walked across the room, dressed
only in her bra. Her ass bounced ripples down the
backs of her legs. It was her way of seizing Pin's
complete attention. She was so jealous of our
relationship lately, always trying to get me to cut
down my discussions with Pin. I knew she was doing
the same thing now, pretending to have come down
to get a book. I watched her deliberately skim
through a few, seemingly oblivious to our presence.

Actually, my presence wouldn't have mattered.
Ursula and I have never thought anything about
standing naked before each other. We did it as kids
and we did it as we grew up. In a sense we
participated in each other's development. I remember staying awake one night with her, both of us
staring at her naked chest to see if we could detect
her breasts growing. She fell asleep before I did. I
thought I saw something happen, but it was so quick
and I was a little bleary-eyed by then, so I wouldn't
swear to it. I told her about it, though, just so she'd
feel bad about falling asleep like that.

I use to stare at her a lot, fascinated by our genetic

14

and blood relationship. I wanted to see what of myself I could find in her.

Ursula has worked in the local library ever since she graduated high school. It's just a little hick-town library, nothing spectacular; but Ursula found a second home there. I used to make a great deal of fun of that, but I've learned to temper my jokes some. For the most part, she ignored them anyway or told me I was jealous. What a laugh. Jealous of that! Even when she said it, she said it with half a heart. She knew I could have had my choice of almost any profession I wanted. I was always a straight-A student in school. It was just that when father and mother died in the car accident and left us all that money, the house and father's lucrative investments, well, I just didn't see the sense in doing anything but what I always wanted to do. I've always wanted to write poetry, mainly a great modern epic poem, a kind of American "Beowulf."

I spent most of my time working on it. At night, Pin, Ursula and I sat in the living room and I read them the day's work. I have a high regard for Pin's opinion of poetry, and Ursula does have a good deal of sensitivity for literature, probably because of her job in the library. Both of them always said I read well. I would get a fire going in the fireplace and we'd all sit around sipping coffee after dinner, and then I'd read what I had written. Ursula's eyes always exploded whenever I hit something she thought was "marvelous." She had that word, "marvelous." Pin simply nodded silently at good things. It wasn't a very emphatic nod, just a slight movement of his head. I always looked up quickly from the paper when I read a part I thought he'd appreciate, and sure enough, there would be that

slight nod. I guess being so close to one another over the years had made us very sensitive to each other's reactions. At times I felt we were almost a part of one another.

Ursula had a "wisp of a body." At least that's the way Mrs. Martin referred to it, but Mrs. Martin was so stout that anyone would have a "wisp of a body" standing next to her. She came once a week to clean the house. It took her a long time, almost all day, to do the place. For the most part, I would stay upstairs and Pin would stay in his room behind the garage. She never went into his room. He wouldn't have tolerated any strangers coming into it. He was so emphatic on that point that I had to actually lock his room from the outside. She asked me about it only once. I told her in very strong, definite terms not to worry herself ever about that room. She shrugged and forgot about it. When she left, I opened his room and brought him out. I guess we really didn't need Mrs. Martin to come in and clean. It was just something I felt my mother would have wanted us to do.

Anyhow, Mrs. Martin thought Ursula had a "wisp of a body." That was because she was long legged and small waisted. She had thin arms and nearly no shoulders, but she was not small breasted. She was very deceptive that way. She insisted on giving that impression to people by wearing these awfully tight bras that squeezed her bosom against her.

"Your sister oughta eat something substantial," Mrs. Martin told me once. "It ain't healthy for someone to be so close to their own bones like that."

I could understand why she felt that way. Ursula's face was lean too. Her skin was wrapped tightly around the sharp chin bone. She had thin lips and

her cheeks were as taut as the skin on a drum. The cheekbones protruded a little. The wideness of her forehead made her eyes appear small and deep, but when you stood next to her, you saw that they weren't small eyes. Ursula thought she was ugly and she was always very critical of her appearance. I did a lot to build up her ego. Too much, if you ask me. However, if she asked me what Pin thought of her, I would say, "Ask him yourself. I don't speak for Pin."

People called me "baby-faced." My hair was such a light brown it could almost be called blonde, which I thought was a genetic mistake. But my father, or rather, Pin, explained it was by no means a "mistake." "Your grandfather on your mother's side was very light haired and had the same kind of milky white skin with tiny freckles in his cheeks and along the sides of his nose. In fact you have your mother's nose and a somewhat soft, feminine mouth."

"Feminine?" I didn't like the way he said that. I was broad shouldered and two inches taller than Ursula. When I was a teenager, I was accused of having a "Van Johnson look," so I didn't really take to this "feminine mouth" thing. I suppose I got too defensive because I said, "Well, you know, you don't have much of a masculine face. Your nose is too straight and too pretty. Your ears are too perfect. And your penis is too small." I thought that would hurt him.

"Penis size has nothing to do with sexual potency," he said. Smugly, of course. I told Ursula what he said and she said size doesn't even have anything to do with sexual gratification. She said she told her girl friends that, but most of them refused to believe it.

17

The three of us lived here in my parents' old house about a quarter of a mile up Hassens Hill in Woodridge, New York. Woodridge is a small village in the Catskills, a little to the left of center of the heart of the Borscht Belt. I like to get anatomical when I describe where it's located. Everyone's always using that expression—"The heart of the Borscht Belt." I suppose they mean center. I don't know where they get that idea from. It's certainly not true geographically.

I have lived here all my life and I had borscht only once. I wasn't crazy about it. Ursula likes it, but doesn't like what it does to her. She says it repeats; so she doesn't eat it. Pin says he could take it or leave it. My father felt the same way about it and my mother didn't like the way it could stain her table-cloths.

The house is a two-story building with an attached garage. The garage was added on years after the house was built. On the bottom level, once you come in, we have our rather large living room with an adjoining dining room. To the left of the dining room is the kitchen. On the right side of the kitchen is a door that leads out to the pantry and from there out to our backyard, a small clearing surrounded by a heavily wooded area with a pond behind it. Ursula and I have walked out to it many times. We have a bathroom downstairs, right off the living room. To the left of the living room is a small bedroom situated behind the garage. This is Pin's room.

Upstairs we have three bedrooms and a bath-room. Ursula's bedroom and my bedroom have an adjoining door. We left our parents' room just the way it was the day they died. We didn't give any of

their clothes away or upset any furniture arrangements. We don't go in there much, and the door is always closed. Our bedrooms have windows that open to the road outside. My room is toward the high side of the hill and Ursula's is toward the low side.

The house has faded white wood shingles with black aluminum shutters. We had the shutters put on recently. We haven't made many improvements on the house; neither of us really takes much interest in what it looks like. Ursula says as long as the heating works and the plumbing works, why worry about it? Pin rarely goes outside, so he couldn't care less about its appearance. People are always coming around or calling up to try to sell us some kind of home improvements. They all know we have money. My father was a very successful doctor here. Practically everyone went to him. His and my mother's funeral was a mob scene.

Once in a while I fooled around with my father's stethoscope and other paraphernalia. I'd take Pin's blood pressure and listen to his heartbeat and he'd do the same to me. When we were kids, Ursula and I always used to listen to each other's heartbeat. We still do sometimes, just for gags. The other night, I remember, we all had a little too much to drink and I took out the old stethoscope, putting it in my ears and walking around the place the way my father used to walk around. Then Ursula took off her blouse and called me over to listen to her heart. It was beating rapidly. I stuck the thing down into her bra and tickled the nipple on her breast. She laughed and screeched. Pin almost fell out of his seat in hysterics. Then she wanted Pin to listen to her

heartbeat. She nearly ripped the earlobes off me, pulling the damn thing away from me, and sauntered over to him. She shoved her breasts in his face and stuck the stethoscope into his ears. It kept falling out. Finally, she had to hold it to his head. He looked at me as if to say, "We've got to humor her when she gets like this." I turned away.

After Ursula drank too much and got silly, she would always get maudlin and cry. I'd have to take her upstairs and help her get undressed and into bed. She would really get helplessly infantile at these times. I guess it all had to do with our losing our parents the way we did. At least, that's the way Pin explained it away. He was very learned and well read on the subject of psychology, and usually pedantic about his knowledge, I might add. I suppose he was right. Whatever the reason, Ursula needed the tenderness and affection. She wouldn't want to wear nightclothes. Naked, she slipped into the bed, sobbing softly and pressing my fingers against her lips. I would sit on the bed and stroke her hair. Sometimes she fell asleep quickly, and sometimes she talked. Usually her conversations centered around the Need and how she reacted to it. It was very intimate talk, but she had no one besides me to confide in.

The Need was one thing my father discussed with us. He had very liberal ideas about sex and he was always very factual and clinical about it. There wasn't a question he wouldn't answer if we had the nerve to ask it, and he loved to make fun of the words and expressions some parents thought up to avoid telling it like it is. One day he sat Ursula and me down in the living room and went through the

whole sexual process. I was two years older than she, of course, but, remarkably, our bodies were coming into maturity at the same time. He used the word "remarkable." He explained sex to us in terms of a biological need. He said that just as people get thirsty for water, they get thirsty for sex. For a long time the sex thirst is very great, and then it gets less and less intense. It's better to know all about it, he said, so you can go about satisfying the Need without hurting yourselves. Ursula sort of got the idea that getting pregnant was hurting herself. Of course, my father tried to correct that misconception later by explaining that pregnancy wasn't physically damaging. He never bothered with the moral or social aspects. In a rare criticism of my father, Pin said he should have bothered.

I'll never forget how my father pronounced the word, "vagina." He said, "vorgina," and looked very intense when he said it. Although his description of an orgasm was very scientific, there was still something mysterious and erotic about it. I'm sure he left us with an impression opposite to his intent. Although we didn't come right out and tell it to each other, we were both dying to experiment with our bodies. I like to think that was normal.

Very soon afterward, Ursula found a book in my father's library that went into it all in very great detail. It was an old book, however, and many of the concepts and theories are outdated today. The thesis of one of the sections was that masturbation is very bad for you. It described all sorts of possible horrible effects, including a drying up of the sexual organs. I think the initial reading and studying of that book definitely had a bad lifelong effect on us. We often

experienced guilt feelings along with any sexual acts. I wanted to discuss the things we read with my father, but it was always very difficult, if not impossible, for either Ursula or me to initiate an intimate conversation with him. He would talk when approached, but he was so aloof and objective that it left us with a cold feeling. Mother would write that off by saying, "It's just the doctor's way."

For the most part, Ursula had the Need more than I did, and that's leaving out the times she went into Pin's room to satisfy the Need with him. At first she wouldn't admit to it, but I knew that was why she went in.

"Your father should have read more Freud," Pin told me. "Then maybe he wouldn't have been so matter of fact about sex. He didn't have the proper respect for sex." I nodded because I had just finished reading some Freud myself.

"I know. There was nothing romantic about my father."

"I don't mean the romantic end of it. I mean the psychological end of it," he said in a very pedantic tone of voice. When Pin was serious, he would tolerate no frivolity.

"I suppose you're right," I said. I was always supposing Pin was right.

As time went by, I noted that it took more and more to satisfy Ursula's Need. There were times when I was tempted to say something about it to my father, but I just couldn't get myself to betray Ursula that way. I knew she would interpret it as a betrayal. We had so many secrets from our parents. For me to go and discuss her sex life with my father, I would have had to breach an unwritten agreement between us. I worried about her, though. I saw the way she

looked at boys in school and I knew how they thought of her.

Once I found our telephone number on the wall in the boys' room. There was a little note under it that said, "If you want an easy screw, Ursula will do." It enraged me and I tried to scrub it off. Finally I had to literally chip the wall away. I brought it to her attention early one evening, but she didn't seem to realize the full import of what was happening.

"Why do you think the boys picked your name out to write on the wall?"

"I don't know. What's the difference? What harm does it do?"

"What harm does it do? WHAT HARM DOES IT DO?" I was beside myself. I felt my face flush. "Jesus, how can you be so damn indifferent!"

I turned and looked at her. She sat there looking down at her hands in her lap. Then, when she realized I wasn't talking, she looked up and smiled stupidly at me.

"Do you want every creep in the school calling you for a date?"

"Oh, nobody will call."

"What makes you so sure, Ursula?" She looked down. "What makes you so sure?"

"I'm sure," she said and she left. I was so mad all I could do was lie down on my bed and stare at the wall. Later she came in and sat next to me. She touched my shoulder, but I didn't turn toward her.

"I guess I can't hide my feelings," she said. "I guess boys see it on my face."

"Well, you better do something about it," I said, "or you'll be unhappy."

"You'll still love me, won't you, Leon? Won't you?"

"I don't know," I said. She was silent for a while. Then I felt her hand on my cheek. I turned and looked up at her. She smiled and, of course, I couldn't stay angry at her much longer. "At least make an effort, will you, Ursula?"

"I'll try," she said. "I'll really try."

Chapter 2

As long as I can remember, Pin has always been with us. He was in my father's office before I was born. As far as I know, my father's voice would come out of himself and out of Pin. People at dinners or at parties would try to get my father to do voice throwing, but he wouldn't. He wouldn't do it anywhere but in the office. When Ursula and I were very small children, we would sit on the floor in the office and listen as my father and Pin carried on conversations about different patients, reviewing diagnosis, treatment and prognosis. Occasionally my father would say something like, "Oh, you don't concur," and then he'd do some more research and discuss the research. Right from the beginning, I had the sense that whenever he was trying to convince

26

Pin of something, he was really trying to convince himself.

As a child I remember staring at Pin's face while my father and he talked. Pin was absolutely inscrutable, except for the smallest gleam in his eyes. Of course, Pin was naked in the office. Being it was a doctor's office, that was all right. When he came to our house later on, we dressed him in my father's clothes. They were practically the same size. But naked, he was certainly fascinating to look at.

His transparent body was soft as skin. All of the internal organs were different colors to correspond with a chart my father had on the wall beside Pin. Each organ was described in terms of its function. The printed matter was done in the same color as the organ. Every one of Pin's joints was movable. Even his diaphragm was movable.

My father used Pin not only when he explained parts of the body to children, but also when he explained ailments to adults. I never saw anyone come away without being fascinated by Pin. Why, the fingers of his hands were as long and as powerful looking as my father's.

Anyway, it was interesting to listen in when my father had these discussions with Pin. Pin was always careful about contradicting him. His tone of voice was always polite. In those days there wasn't the slightest trace of temper in his tone. He never raised his voice.

Occasionally, my father would stop in the middle of a discussion and stare at him. I'd wait with my little hands folded neatly in my lap, my breathing subdued, and look from him to Pin and back to him again. Pin never changed expression. The more I think about it, I don't see how my father could have

realized Pin was disagreeing. That's why I say my father was really out to convince himself. If he had doubts, he would assume Pin had them.

My father wouldn't talk to Pin much when adults were being treated, but he often did when he treated children. He'd look over at Pin propped up in the corner and he'd say, "Guess what we have here?" Pin would reply, "What?" The child's eyes would grow big, but my father wouldn't crack a smile. He was always serious, even when he talked to Pin in front of children. "We have a bad throat infection," he'd answer, or he'd say, "Another stomach flu. It's a regular epidemic."

One time when I was waiting for my father in the lobby, I had to go to the bathroom bad. He let me through the examination room just before a senior high-school girl, Maralyn Meyers, came in. I was in the bathroom so long, I guess my father forgot I was there. When I was finished, I opened the door slowly and looked out before walking back through the office. Maralyn Meyers was naked from the waist down and she was up on the examination table, her feet stuck in what I later found out were called stirrups. My father was giving her an internal examination, but I thought he was helping her because she had gotten the Need. Pin was sitting in his corner, just behind my father. He didn't say a word. He just sat gazing straight ahead. When he spotted me, a faint smile formed on his face and I was afraid he was going to laugh at me, so I closed the bathroom door and waited. When I opened it again, Maralyn was gone and my father was outside talking to Miss Sansodome, his secretary. I came out and walked over to the desk. I looked down and read the things my father had written about Maralyn

Meyers. I read them quickly, as much of it as I could make out.

"The doctor forgot about me in there, I guess," I said to Pin.

"He's got a lot on his mind, Leon. You did the right thing waiting in the bathroom. It might have been embarrassing for Maralyn Meyers."

"Maralyn Meyers is a pretty girl. I know a lot of boys like her."

"I know," Pin said. He was smiling for sure now. "I think too many boys like her or she likes too many boys."

"You mean, she has the Need a lot?"

"Oh, a lot. But she's going to have to forget about the Need for a while. She has a broken ovary."

"I know all about ovaries," I said with some pride. "The doctor explained it all to Ursula and me."

"I know," Pin said. Just then my father reentered.

"Leon, what are you doing here now? I want you to wait outside or in the lobby."

"I was in the bathroom and I came out to talk to Pin."

"Well, forget about talking to Pin. I've got two more people to see yet."

"OK."

"Besides," he said looking from Pin to me suspiciously, "I've told you before. I don't like you coming in here to talk to Pin."

"You talk to him," I said quickly. I said the same thing to him the last time he warned me about it.

"That's only out of habit, years of habit. For me it's one thing. The patients get a kick out of it. It relaxes them and it helps with the children who come in here, but with you . . ."

"It relaxes me too," I said sullenly. "If it's all right

for you, it's all right for me," I said again. I shot a glance at Pin. He was diplomatically quiet at these times, but I thought he was amused by my courage and quick mind. Not many people could stand up to my father, especially not my mother. All he'd have to do is glare at her and she'd shut up.

"I haven't the time to discuss it now," he said, turning me by the shoulder and heading me toward the door. I snapped my head to the right quickly.

"So long, Pin," I said deliberately. My father's fingers tightened around the back of my neck. He surprised me with the pain.

"Wait outside," he shouted.

I don't know why my father was so sensitive about my relationship with Pin, unless he was jealous of it. That might explain it. Now, in the beginning, he used to think Ursula's relationship with Pin was cute. She'd sit on Pin's lap and cuddle up to him, placing his right hand on her knees and his left on her shoulder. Once father found her asleep in Pin's lap like that. Occasionally he would threaten her at the dinner table and tell her if she didn't eat her vegetables, he would tell Pin not to ever talk to her again. He never told her it was silly to visit with Pin. He even came home on her birthday once with two gifts—one he said came from him, and the other he said came from Pin. Finally I asked him about it.

We were alone in the car, coming back from the office. He was his usual quiet self, thinking his thousand thoughts, as my mother used to say. Sometimes he'd pass a whole day without saying more than a few words to her. I looked in Rosenblatt's Department Store window and saw a naked manikin being dressed in a new outfit.

"How come you don't mind Ursula's talking to Pin, but you mind me?"

"Ursula's just a little girl. Little girls are always playing with dolls, talking to them and treating them like real people. They feed them, they clothe them, they sing to them. That's what it means to be a little girl."

"I know lots of boys who play with dolls," I said quickly, and I kept opening and closing my left hand. The fingers always got numb when my father, and, later, my mother, threatened my relationship with Pin. One time when my father bawled me out about it, I sat perfectly still, taking on Pin's posture and Pin's expression. I held my head just as stiffly and I didn't say a word to him, even when he asked me questions. After he left me, I remained that way for at least fifteen minutes, and when I did loosen up, it took almost an hour for me to get my hands warm again. My Uncle Hymie always said I was a stubborn child. Maybe that explains it. I don't like to think too much about it.

My father didn't like my analogy to little boys who played with dolls. "You're not a little boy," he said, "you're a little man." Sometimes I think he wanted me to skip childhood completely. Instead of giving me comic books, he gave me *Compton's Picture Encyclopedia*. Instead of giving me children's records, he brought home an album of beginner's French.

He was always trying to get me ahead. I found out he went to the school to request they give me tests to see if I couldn't be skipped a grade. He thought I scored high enough on the tests, but the principal didn't. He went to the board of education, but they

backed up the principal. Because of that and some other things he did, the teachers treated me like a freak. He didn't do any of this for Ursula. Ursula was just a normal little girl as far as he was concerned. He let her read nursery rhymes and didn't think it was necessary for her to get ahead. Any silly thing she did was all right. In fact, she was the one who gave Pin his name, according to my mother, and they found it amusing.

"The first time the doctor showed her the inside of his office and she met Pin, she baptized him Pinocchio."

"I wouldn't want anybody calling me Pinocchio," I said. I admit I was a little jealous. If I would have done it, they wouldn't have thought it amusing. I asked Pin about it once.

"Don't you mind Ursula calling you Pinocchio?"

"Well . . ."

"What if I called you Pinocchio?"

"It is somewhat unusual. I guess it's the kind of thing a silly little girl would think of."

"I'm not going to call you Pinocchio. I'm going to call you Pin."

"That's fine."

"I'll tell Ursula to call you Pin, too," I said.

Of course, Ursula did. She did most anything I told her to do, especially if I said Pin agreed. That was because she was much more dependent on me than I was on her. All I had to do was threaten to ignore her and she'd give in. For the longest time, we only had each other to play with. My father didn't want anyone in the house when he came home from work. He was adamant about that. There weren't many kids who really wanted to come to our house anyway. My mother was too discouraging and very

obvious about her displeasure if someone was brought home.

"You'll have to take off your shoes and leave them by the door there," she'd say. "Don't run your hands on the walls like kids are always doing. I don't need the hours of work to take off the greasy prints. And anything you take out to play with must be put back immediately afterward. I'm not going to go about picking up after you kids."

She looked at them with such a wild-eyed rage that most anyone who stepped in our door was eager to get back out. I suppose my father should have paid more attention to her problems. He was so wrapped up in himself and his work, though; he just ignored it. She could be on her hands and knees scrubbing the same spot on the tiles in the entranceway and he'd walk in, hang up his coat, take the paper and sit down in the living room. Once she rubbed the inside of a window so hard she pushed it right out of the frame, splattering glass on the ground outside. A jagged edge cut her arm and he put in a few stitches, treating her just as though she were any patient off the street.

When I was older, I asked him about her. "Don't you think there's something wrong with Mom? I mean the way she cleans, the time she spends boiling the silverware and everything?"

My father didn't respond. He turned the page of his magazine as though I hadn't even spoken. I deliberately stood there in front of him, waiting. I would make him recognize me, make him consider my question. After a while he did look up.

"Why don't you ask Pin about it?" he said, looking at the magazine again. I was stunned. I blushed and felt ridiculous. That was cruel, I

thought, that was damn cruel. It was my mother, his wife. Didn't he care?

I gave up, and I gave up on bringing anyone home with me too. Ursula avoided it for the longest time as well; and when you don't invite kids to your house, they don't invite you to theirs. That was why we spent so much time down at my father's office. It was the only real opportunity we had to meet other kids after school and on weekends, even though those kids were suffering from colds or the flu or whatever. Ursula did have a girl friend over once, Miriam Cohen, but Miriam's mother never let her come again.

Ursula had spent four days whining and crying until my mother gave in and permitted her to invite Miriam over.

"I want promises. I want things kept clean. I want things picked up. I don't want anyone here who's getting a cold or who isn't clean."

"Why don't we just sterilize her at the door," I said. My mother slapped me across the face. She rarely struck either of us, so it was quite a shock, even though it only stung for a moment. My mother's hands were boney and worn looking probably from handling all that detergent. It was like being struck by a skeleton. Ursula thought I ruined it for her, but my mother pulled her hand to herself and turned to Ursula.

"Remember what I told you," she said, which was her way of saying, "All right."

Miriam came on a Saturday morning. Her father drove her over. I was sitting in my room looking out the window when she got out of the car. Miriam was a tall, thin girl with dark brown hair cut short. Her

mouth drooped a little at the corners, giving her an habitually sad expression. I think she was an unhappy girl anyway. She was all legs and had a tiny pouch of a belly that sagged and protruded when she wore those tight-fitting slacks girls were wearing. Her complexion was a sickly looking white. I diagnosed her as anemic, but Pin didn't think it was necessarily true.

Some of the girls in Ursula's class, including Ursula, had already started developing breasts, but one look at Miriam Cohen would tell you that this girl was going to be a late bloomer. I knew why Ursula liked her. It was because no one else paid any attention to her and she was grateful for Ursula's attention. If Ursula didn't sit with her in the cafeteria during lunch, no one did.

As soon as Miriam entered the house, my mother was at the door warning both of them to stay in Ursula's room and be sure not to disturb anything in any of the other rooms. She told them that if they wanted to, they could come down for cookies and milk in about an hour. I was surprised at that because she hated it when Ursula and I ate cookies. We'd drop too many crumbs about. I used to eat cookies over the sink and then run the water to wash the sides down with a sponge.

Actually, my mother's cleaning energy was a phenomenon. She was such a thin, fragile-looking woman. She surely burned a day's calories merely worrying about the house. The furniture was kept spotlessly clean because she kept plastic covers draped over the chairs and the couches most of the day. I hated sitting on them. We rarely ate in the dining room. She claimed that was for special

occasions. My father didn't seem to mind. I often wondered how they ever made love. Pin said she washed his prick down with Spic and Span. It was one of the funniest things Pin ever said.

Ursula and I spent about ninety percent of our indoor time in our rooms. We each had a small color television set to keep us contained and out of the rest of the house. Mother had a schedule. On Mondays she would come up and clean Ursula's room and Ursula would have to spend her time in mine. On Tuesdays she cleaned my room and I spent my time in Ursula's. It always took me a day or two to get used to moving around in my own room after my mother left it.

Miriam and Ursula were sent right upstairs to her room. I went back into mine and sat by the adjoining door listening to their conversation. They talked low about boys in school and their teachers. They talked for a long time. It was like they had first met each other or something. Neither of them could wait to get her thoughts out to the other. Sometimes they talked at the same time. Eventually Ursula introduced the Need as a topic of conversation. I was expecting her to do that. From the way Miriam listened and responded, it was evident that she hadn't much information about it. She kept asking Ursula questions and Ursula answered them like a little sex education instructor or something. She took on the pedantic, correct tone of voice that father often had. Their voices got lower and lower, and after a while, I didn't hear a thing. I thought for a moment that they had gone down for cookies and milk, so I went out and quietly made my way to the kitchen. But my mother was alone in there, polish-

ing silverware. I quickly made my way back up to my room and listened at the door again. There was hardly a sound. I knew they wouldn't have the nerve to go anywhere else in the house.

Slowly and very carefully, I turned the knob of the door. I must have spent ten minutes turning it. When I felt it would open, I moved it back by fractions of an inch until there was just a slight crack of an opening there. Then I sprawled out on the floor and peeked through it. At first I saw nothing; just an empty room. Then I saw both of them, lying naked on the bed. They were just lying there, side by side, staring up at the ceiling. I watched them like that for the longest time. Then I saw Miriam turn toward Ursula and sort of shrug her shoulders.

"I don't feel anything," she said. "Are you sure this works?" Ursula had a smile on her face and looked a little flushed. She put her finger to her lips to indicate that Miriam should be silent and then she took Miriam's hand and placed it right between Miriam's legs. There was very little hair there and it looked as white as chalk. Ursula kept her hand on Miriam's and she began moving Miriam's hand in small, circular rubbing motions.

She did this for quite a while, but Miriam didn't seem to have any response. Ursula was getting impatient with her. Finally Ursula took her hand off and put it on herself. Miriam just lay there watching Ursula work herself up. I thought the expression on Miriam's face was very funny, but I held in any laughter. Then Ursula had Miriam turn over on her stomach, her hands under her and between her legs. Ursula moved Miriam up and down on her own hands by pushing slowly and firmly on her naked ass.

They did this for quite a while too. Ursula looked like she was getting angrier and angrier. Finally, I could take it no longer myself.

I opened the door further and slipped into the bedroom. I was halfway up to the bed, crawling, when Ursula saw me. I put my hand up to indicate that she shouldn't say anything and she didn't. I knew she would cooperate. She just sat there looking down at me while Miriam continued working on herself. When I got to the bed, I took Ursula's hand off of Miriam's ass and did it myself. I helped her along the way Ursula had been doing. At least two minutes must have gone by before Ursula couldn't hold in her laughter any longer. When she did laugh, Miriam turned and sat up.

The moment she saw me, she screamed and covered her nipples with her hands. I fell back on the floor and rolled around, laughing hysterically, while Miriam rushed around the room gathering her clothes. She was sobbing at this point, so I got up and went back into my own room. A little while later, I heard Miriam and Ursula leave and go downstairs. And then, not long after that, Miriam's father came back up the hill and picked her up. My mother didn't know what had happened and she didn't care. She was grateful that Miriam was leaving, I guess. After she was gone, Ursula came up to my room.

"You're a bastard," she said. "You did that just because I had a friend over and you didn't."

"You played along."

"I didn't know what else to do," she said walking to the window. There was a moment of silence between us. Ursula couldn't stay angry at me long.

"Leon, why do you suppose the Need isn't so great in Miriam?"

"I don't know. Ask the doctor. He'll be glad to tell you all about it."

"He'll start asking me all kinds of questions if I do."

"So ask Pin," I said. She turned around fast and stared at me for a moment.

"Do you still ask Pin a lot of things, Leon?"

"Why?"

"I just wondered. I heard the doctor and mother talking about you and Pin. They don't like the way you talk about him all the time."

"That's tough."

"They blamed each other."

"For what?"

"For letting it go on, between Pin and us. I don't think we'll be able to talk about Pin in front of them anymore, Leon."

"You're probably right."

"We'll keep him to ourselves, huh?" There was some new excitement in her eyes. She walked over and sat on my bed. "I mean, we won't ever mention his name in front of them anymore, OK?"

"I suppose so."

"I think Pin is a very lonely person," she said. Her tone of voice indicated she wanted to play one of those create-your-own-world games. I wasn't in the mood, and besides, Pin wasn't a toy. "I think he wishes he could live here with us. What do you think?"

"Yes," I said. "I think he does."

"Miriam Cohen isn't half as pretty as I am, is she, Leon? Not half as pretty." She looked at herself in

my dresser mirror and stroked her hair. I thought about what she had said about keeping Pin a secret. The idea made my heart beat faster. I was afraid, afraid of . . . losing him.

It made my fingers numb again. Ursula saw me opening and closing them.

"What's the matter with your hand?"

"Nothing," I said quickly. She reached out and took my hands into hers. I looked into her smiling face and the numbness seemed to go away.

Chapter 3

URSULA WAS FOURTEEN YEARS OLD WHEN FATHER PER-
formed the abortion. I knew she was having sex with
boys. She told me all about it. That was an effect
father had on us, I guess. We were both very
matter-of-fact with each other about things other
brothers and sisters kept very private and personal.
We got into the habit of sitting together in the dark
of our rooms, after a night out with someone, and
discussing it. If I went out, she would be waiting up
for me in my room. And if she went out, I was either
waiting in her room, or in my own with the adjoining
door wide open.

One particular night she came in about a quarter
to eleven. She was permitted to stay out until

midnight and most always she stayed out right to twelve, so I was surprised to hear her walking up the stairs. The light went on in her room and I walked in rather than wait for her to come to me this time. She was standing in front of the dresser mirror, combing her hair harshly with a metal comb. I watched her for a while. She was obviously very agitated.

"OK, what's the matter?" I said, taking a seat on her bed.

"Everything."

"That narrows it down perfectly. Didn't you go out with Mike Elias tonight?" Elias was in my class and he was always telling me how much he admired my sister. He buttered me up a lot. I was very indifferent to him, sometimes downright rude, but he ignored or took everything I dished out.

"Yes," she said, unbuttoning her blouse. I saw a red streak down the back of her neck. It looked like a scrape of some sort.

"What happened here?" I said, getting up and touching it.

"He was a bit clumsy in the 'throes of passion.' How do you like that expression? Shirley Bennet showed it to me in a book today. 'The throes of passion.'" Her lips grew tight and she squinted her eyes as if she were about to break out in tears.

"Beautiful. What really happened?"

"That's what happened," she said, with a little laugh following her as she hung the blouse up in the closet. She unzipped her skirt and stepped out of it.

"Where did you go with him?"

"Where you went with Cora two nights ago, Kaplan's Lake. It was a great spot—dark road to the lake, and parking there with the moonlight dancing on the water. Isn't that the way you put it?"

"You went there just because I went there, didn't you?"

"You know good spots are hard to find. Mike always wants to go to the cemetery and I don't feel comfortable there."

"Shit."

"What's the matter, Leon?" she asked with a sly smile on her face. I watched her reach back and unfasten her bra. Her breasts shook for an instant and then stabilized in their firmness. At fourteen, Ursula had the bosom of a fully grown woman. She turned around and reached up for her nightgown.

"So? What happened to make you so upset and bring you home early?" I waited as she went out to the bathroom to brush her teeth and wash her face. I didn't like the way she was avoiding me. It wasn't like her. Usually she was eager to discuss her dates and get my opinions. The first night she let a boy put his hand on her naked breasts, she came home and we lay together on her bed in the dark. She spoke softly, telling me how it sent electricity through her body.

"He had his leg between mine," she told me, "and I felt him pressing against my vagina."

"Vorgina," I said. It was automatic.

"I liked it. We got into a kind of rhythm. I had two orgasms."

"What about him?" I said dryly.

"I don't know. I wasn't interested in what he had. Are girls interested in what you have?"

"Sometimes. Cora Brooks is always asking me how it feels. She drives me nuts that way. I keep telling her to shut up and she keeps asking me how it feels. I think she's keeping some secret statistics."

"I can see where that would be annoying."

So it was very unusual for Ursula to be close-mouthed about her dates. When she came out of the bathroom, I asked her again.

"What upset you tonight?"

"I went to the brink," she said, getting into bed, "and I lost control."

"What do you mean?"

"Remember how I'm always telling you how much control I think I have because I'm so aware of my body and its reactions to things?"

"So?"

"I don't have it."

"Are you going to make sense or not? If you don't want to talk, it's perfectly all right with me," I said, and started for the door.

"Don't get so uptight. It isn't easy this time."

"OK," I said, turning back. "OK." I was quiet. I sat back on her bed and leaned against the wall, waiting.

"We had intercourse," she finally said. I closed my eyes hard when she said it. I remember doing that, but I don't know why. I didn't say anything even though she paused for a few moments. "I remembered what you told me about Cora getting excited when you spent all that time kissing her shoulder. It sounded good somehow. I got him to do it to me. He was impatient, but I kept him at it."

She paused again. I thought about Mike Elias, a tall, lean redhead with milk-white skin. He had freckles scattered over his neck and forehead. He wouldn't be bad-looking except for some missing teeth.

You could see he was aware of it because he rarely

gave anyone a wide smile and had the habit of mumbling a lot. He didn't open his mouth enough to voice sounds clearly.

"We were in the back of his car," she went on. "He had his hand between my legs too. I just felt like I was going to explode if I didn't do something to stop the pounding of my heart. Do you know what I mean, Leon? Do you know what I mean?"

"Yes," I said. I didn't look at her when I said it, though. She went on.

"I took my bra off myself. Just the way Cora did. You said that had a big effect on you. He kept kissing my breasts, my nipples, between my breasts, working his way down my body with his lips. That was wild, Leon. Did you ever do that? Huh?"

"No. Yes. I don't remember."

"What got me was . . ."

"What?"

"He kept kissing me further and further down. My skirt and panties slipped off and I felt his lips there. I sat back with my right leg up on the back of the front seat. I heard him take his pants off. I couldn't think. I had gone beyond thought. Did you ever get that way, Leon?"

"Stop asking me questions."

"I'm just trying to explain."

"So. Just explain."

"Leon, I just opened up to him. There was no resistance, no control. He was wild and clumsy and sloppy. That's when he scratched my neck. I bawled him out afterward," she said, giggling, but it was a very nervous-sounding giggle. "You should have seen that." She giggled again. I felt her reach out and touch my shoulder, but I didn't look at her. "Leon?"

46

"What?"

"Are you listening to me?"

"Yes."

"You're mad at me, aren't you?"

"Why should I be mad at you? It's your body. If that's what you wanted and he's the one you wanted it with . . . besides, remember what the doctor said: 'If you're hungry, you eat.'"

"Do you really think he meant *this?* I mean, do you actually think he meant for us to have intercourse now?"

"Why not?" I was surprised at the high pitch my voice took. I sounded like Pin.

"Should I do it again?"

"It's up to you."

"I was thinking about asking the doctor for birth control pills. I figure that would be a good way to see just how serious he was when he told us sex was just another Need, another physiological Need, as he called it."

"I don't think I totally agree with that, but if the doctor said it . . . are you really going to ask for pills?"

"I thought I'd go to the office one day and sort of ask him through Pin, know what I mean? It'll be easier. He'll answer through Pin. I'm sure of it. You told him about your intercourse with Beverly Steine through Pin, didn't you?"

"No. I just told Pin," I said. She didn't say anything for a while. I felt her hand travel down until she found mine on the bed. We remained like that in the darkness until I got tired and went to sleep in my own bed. She was disappointed that I didn't stay with her longer.

Ursula never asked father for the birth-control

pills. She said she didn't have the nerve.

"I stood in front of Pin for a couple of minutes, but I couldn't get myself to do it."

"Why not?"

"I felt . . . silly."

I didn't laugh, but she knew what I thought of that. I was also well aware of how many times she went out with Elias after the first night they had intercourse. (I always wanted to say "screwed" or "fucked," but father's terminology was most influential. I knew the other guys laughed behind my back when I used the word "penis" for "prick," or "vorgina" for "cunt.") Ursula wanted to describe each date to me, but I started acting bored and disinterested. She was always eager to hear about my dates, though. One night I told her I was taking Miriam Cohen to the drive-in. We were doubling up with Tony Martin, who had a station wagon.

"How could she go out with you? Every time I look at her in school, I think of that day when you snuck in on us and played with her ass."

"She's forgotten, I guess. Or else the memory excites her."

"But she's so ugly and she has that bad acne all over her forehead and on her neck."

"I can handle it." My revelation was having just the effect I thought it would have on Ursula.

"You must be getting desperate. What's the matter with Cora?"

"I'm tired of her."

"Are you really attracted to Miriam Cohen?"

"Every girl is a new adventure for me."

"Bullshit," Ursula said. "I don't believe you."

"Suit yourself."

When I came home that night, she was waiting for me in my room. I know she heard me come in, but she pretended to be asleep in my bed. I went to the bathroom, got undressed, slipped on pajama bottoms and came out. She was still lying there with her eyes closed. So I sat on the bed and acted as though I didn't even notice her. When I slipped under the covers, she opened her eyes and stretched.

"What time is it?"

"One-fifteen."

"How was your date with Miriam?" she asked, sitting up quickly. As usual, she had crawled under my covers naked.

"Very bad. She was a virgin."

"Don't tell me you didn't expect that."

"Let's just say I had my suspicions."

"So?" She was waiting for me to go on, but I didn't respond. "What didja do?"

"I was going ahead with it anyway, but when I got between her naked thighs, I found pimples all over the inside of her legs, right up to her crotch."

"Ugh. I think I'm going to be sick," she said, holding her stomach. I laughed.

"So I went out and bought two portions of hot buttered popcorn."

"Serves you right."

"I wouldn't talk," I said, but I regretted saying it almost immediately. I don't know why I said it. She was quiet for a few moments. Then she spoke up.

"Leon?"

"What?"

"I'm scared about something."

"What?"

49

"I haven't had my period. It's more than three weeks late."

"You're kidding."

"I wish I was."

"Holy shit," I said, sitting up quickly.

"Remember what the doctor told us," she said. "It's not a hundred-percent certainty."

"Yeah, but . . . what are you going to do?"

"I don't know. Wait a little longer, I guess." She rested her head on the pillow and pulled the covers up to her neck.

"Holy shit."

"Stop saying that, damnit." I lay back again too. We were both staring up at the ceiling. "I guess I should have had the nerve to ask the doctor for the pills, huh?"

"I guess so, or at least been more careful. You'll hafta tell him."

"I just . . . can't."

"You'll hafta. The longer you wait, the worse it can be," I said. I had the craziest thought going through my head. I imagined that my father would blame me for her pregnancy. I imagined that he knew all about us and our intimate conversations. He'd find out through Pin. The thought made me sweat.

"Leon, the doctor's done an abortion in his office. I know he has."

"How did you find out? And don't say Pin told you," I added quickly.

"I wasn't going to say that. I read something on his desk," she said after a moment's hesitation. If father ever found that out, he'd be enraged.

"I suppose you also read who it was."

50

"Yes. It was that fat Lillian Rogers, the woman who has five kids and lives on the other side of Glen Wild in that old, broken-down-looking house. Her husband probably made her get it."

"Right in the office?"

"Yes."

"I guess there's not that much to it then."

"There's going to be only one way to find out."

"Do you think he would tell mother?"

"No."

He didn't, either. Another week passed and the second one had started when Ursula told father. She went over to his office and waited out in the lobby for him just like any other patient. I walked over with her, but I didn't have the nerve to hang around when she told him. I ran all the way home and waited for her in my room. It seemed like hours before she came back.

"He's going to do it Sunday," she said, "when the office is closed."

"How did he . . . what did he say when you first told him?"

"He listened and asked me questions just like he would ask anyone questions. It gave me the creeps. I almost felt like paying Miss Sansodome when I finally left. He's having a quick test done, but there's little doubt."

"He must've said something. What'd he say?"

"Nothing. He tinkered with his dumb instruments. I turned to Pin and I talked to him. I kept saying, 'I'm sorry, Pin. Please forgive me, Pin. I'm sorry.'" She started to cry so I got up and put my arm around her and walked her back into her own room to sit on her own bed.

"It'll be all right."

"I wish he had yelled at me or looked disappointed, at least. I almost feel like telling mother."

"What for?"

"Just to get a reaction."

"It bothers him. It's just that he doesn't like to show it."

"I don't think so. What bothers him, if anything, is that he's got to be in the office on Sunday." I nodded. What could I say? Father cherished his days off. He really did.

Father went to the office first that Sunday. I accompanied Ursula. Mother didn't know a thing about it. He looked a little surprised that I had come along too. I stood there in the doorway with her while he made his preparations. We looked at Pin and Pin looked at us, but we didn't say anything to him. It was father who started talking to him.

"No education like the real thing, eh, Pin?" he said. "This is where it's at, as the kids say nowadays. I took my time explaining sex to them, gave them a better start than I had; but where did it get me, huh? It got me a Sunday in the office." He turned around and looked at us. "OK, come on in, Ursula. Leon? Are you going to observe?"

"No, sir."

"Might be educational."

Ursula was close to tears. She took my hand firmly in hers and I was afraid she would never let go. I shook my head.

"OK, then," he said. "You can go out and close the door. Read a magazine." I nodded.

When I stepped out and turned around to close

the door, father had just taken Ursula by the hand and was gently but firmly leading her to the table. I closed the door. My heart was beating very fast. I felt a little shaky. But the thing that surprised me the most was the tear that had made its way down my cheek to the corner of my mouth.

Chapter 4

URSULA STAYED IN BED FOR A COUPLE OF DAYS AFTER-
ward. My father told my mother that she was having
a bad time with her menstruation. Mother brought
food up to her, but Ursula ate very little. Most of the
time she lay in bed staring up at the ceiling. When I
came home, I tried talking to her, but she didn't
answer much. Then on the third morning, she just
got up and went to school as if nothing had
happened. From that day, though, until she brought
Stanley home, she never went out with boys. It was
quite a drastic reversal. Mother didn't seem to notice
or care and father was always too busy with his
profession to really take an interest. He never really
knew much about her dates when she did go out with
boys.

For a long time afterward, she didn't have the Need, or if she did, she kept it bottled up inside her. I asked her about it a number of times, but she just shrugged. I really was very worried about her. Pin and I talked over the situation. I thought she was heading for some kind of mental breakdown. What I used to do was go over to father's office at night. I had one of his keys. And I'd sit in the dark on the floor at Pin's feet and talk. I asked Ursula to come with me all the time, but she always refused. The only time she couldn't refuse was the night mother and father were killed.

Ralph Wilson, one of the local policemen, called at two in the morning. I wasn't sleeping, but Ursula was.

"Your parents have been in a bad accident, Leon."

"How bad?"

"Pretty bad. I'll be over to your house in a few minutes to explain all of it. You and your sister want to be up."

"I am up."

"Be right there," he said. After he hung up, I went into Ursula's room and woke her up. I had to keep repeating things because she was in such a daze.

"What do you mean, accident?"

"Accident, accident. Don't you know what accident means? They didn't slip on the ice. They're in a car. There must've been a crash."

"Oh, my God." She finally got up and got her robe on. We went downstairs and waited for Ralph Wilson.

He took his hat off as soon as he walked through the front entrance. I thought that was overly dramat-

ic. I've known Ralph Wilson all my life and it seemed very strange for him to be acting so formal with us. Ursula stood to the side, squeezing her body with her folded arms. She looked utterly ridiculous. Ralph directed all of it to me. I think he was afraid to look at Ursula.

"It was a head-on crash on the Olympic Hill. You know that lousy turn, so many accidents."

"Are they . . ." Ursula had her fingers against her mouth.

"The car just doesn't have any front left to it," Ralph said. He was circling the point, but I didn't mind. "No one could have lived through that. The front seat is pushed right into the back. We have to do all sorts of cutting to get the . . . to get them out."

"Oh, my God." Ursula took my arm. I just stared at Ralph.

"I'm sorry," he said.

"Who hit them?"

"Two drunken bastards. Neither of them are seriously hurt. Isn't it always that way? I suppose you'd want us to contact Garfield's Mortuary. I can do that for you."

"Yes, of course."

"I can't tell you how sorry we all feel. This is a great loss for the community."

"Thank you," I said. Ursula turned and ran up the stairs.

"If there's anything we can do . . ."

"I'll let you know."

He nodded, put his hat on and left. I stood there for a few minutes trying to understand that the world would change for us. The most dominant thing I could recall, however, was the great urge to see the

accident, to see how badly they had been mangled, to see the expressions on their faces. I imagined my father would have been terribly annoyed, and my mother would have been absolutely terrified that her clothing would get dirty.

When I went back upstairs, I found Ursula sitting on her bed, her knees up, her arms around her legs, her head against the tops of her knees. Her eyes were closed and she looked asleep.

"Ursula."

Her eyelids twitched and opened slowly.

"I'm so scared," she said.

"It's all right. It'll be all right. We'll cope. Get dressed."

"Dressed? For what? Do you know what time it is? We don't have to identify the bodies or anything like that, do we?" she asked, her eyes getting bigger.

"No, no."

"Then why?"

"We have to go to the office and tell Pin."

"Tell Pin? Pin?"

"Yes, he'll hafta know. It'll be better if we go together, now."

"Leon, no."

"Get dressed," I said and went to my room. She came to the doorway and watched me take my pants out of the closet.

"Leon, don't you understand what's happened? We can't go off to the office now to talk to . . . Leon, please, I don't want to be here alone."

"Get dressed," I said without looking at her. She saw how serious I was about going and finally went to her closet and put on a skirt and blouse. We didn't talk on the way to the office, but all the while I was aware of how she was staring at me. When we got

59

there, Pin knew immediately that something was wrong.

"There's been an accident," I said, "a terrible, terrible accident." Pin waited for the details. Ursula walked around and around the office, touching things. I just sat at Pin's feet, and I described Ralph Wilson's phone call and visit.

"I just can't believe it," Pin said. "I always thought of your father as being indestructible—immortal, somehow. God, the man never even had a cold," Pin added in that same nasal tone father used whenever he spoke through Pin.

"It's hard to believe he's dead, yes."

"Leon, please, let's go home now," Ursula said. I turned and looked at her. She was obviously terrified.

"We'll hafta call Uncle Hyman and Aunt Dorothy," I said.

"Not yet. Let's go home and do it."

"No, we'd better do it now, from here." I went to the phone and made the first call to Uncle Hyman. His wife answered and she was very confused. The sleepiness in her voice amused me. It took her awhile to understand who was calling.

"It's Leon, your nephew," I said twice. Actually, I wasn't surprised by her failure to recognize my voice. We very rarely saw or spoke to each other.

"Leon? Oh, Leon. What do you want? My God, Leon. It's only five-fifty in the morning."

"Is it? Oh yes, it is."

"What's wrong? What is it?" She was really waking up now. I could hear my uncle mumbling in the background, trying to get the receiver away from her. I knew she wouldn't give it to him. She was the

type who had to be the first to know anything. I covered the receiver and turned to Pin.

"She's such a creep. I can just see her in that bed with curlers in her head and chin straps. She's always getting those facials. I don't think you ever met her, did you?"

"Can't recall her."

"Yes, Aunt Sadie, it is only five-fifty in the morning. I'm sorry I had to call you so early, but, you see, there's been a bad accident and my mother and father are dead."

Ursula stuffed her hand against her mouth when I said that. Then she sat in a chair quickly. Aunt Sadie screamed and my uncle grabbed the receiver. He was shouting back at me because she couldn't talk.

"What is it? What? Sadie, be quiet. Leon, this is Uncle Hymie, what is it? What did you tell Aunt Sadie? Leon?"

I smiled at Pin, who seemed to be smiling back. I knew how much my father despised Uncle Hymie.

"I told her there's been a car accident. I told her my mother and my father were killed. It happened to-night." He was silent, but I could hear Aunt Sadie sobbing. It had such an artificial sound to it.

"Where are you and Ursula?" he asked.

"We're at father's office with Pin."

"With who?"

"Pin," I said. "A friend." I looked at Ursula, but she was now standing with her back to me, looking out the window.

"Well, listen," he said, "I'm getting up right now and starting out for Woodridge. You two go home and wait for me there."

"We'll be home by the time you arrive."

"Did you call your Aunt Dot?"

"Not yet. I was about to."

"I can do it," he said.

"Thanks," I said. Ursula turned around. "He's going to call Aunt Dot." She nodded. "See ya later, Uncle Hymie," I said, and hung up. "He won't be here for a few hours."

"What do you think will happen to us now, Leon?" Ursula asked.

"What'dya mean, happen? Nothing."

"How are we gonna live? I mean, don't you think we'll hafta go and live with Uncle Hymie or Aunt Dot?"

"Hell, no. I'm eighteen. I ain't living with either of those two..Jesus, no."

"You're legally on your own," Pin added.

"Yeah, that's right, I'm legally on my own." I looked at Ursula. She stood with her hand on her mouth. "But Ursula's only sixteen."

"Won't they let us stay together?"

"I don't know. Let's worry about that later. We'll be all right."

"If you don't go with them, I won't," she said. I went back over and sat at Pin's feet. "I won't," she repeated.

"I still can't believe your father's actually dead," Pin said.

"The doctor never kissed me," I said. "I can't ever remember him kissing me. I can't even remember my mother kissing me very much."

"He kissed you," Ursula said.

"When?"

"He must've. Sometime or another," she said, and came over to sit beside me.

"He just wasn't a very emotional man," Pin said. "It was part of his way of life to be impersonal. How could he be a doctor and be emotional?"

"Doctors have to be scientifically detached. I know. I always told myself that. He wanted me to be that way, too."

"He was just trying to protect you," Pin said. "Make you strong enough to face hardships, hardships like the one you're facing now."

"Once a woman came to our house with an oozing, pussy sore. It was running down her neck. When I think about it now, I get nauseous. I stood in the room while he treated her and he didn't chase me away. I was only about six, but I remember it vividly."

"It didn't bother him, so he forgot it might bother you, that's all."

"He knew I was there. He wanted me to see it. That was his way."

"I know what you mean," Ursula said.

We were all quiet for a moment and then I thought of something funny. "Mother's going to clean up heaven as soon as she gets there."

"Yeah," Ursula said and giggled. It was a thin strain of a sound. "She'll tell God to take off His shoes."

"Yeah," I said. We both laughed and laughed. Pin didn't laugh. He stared ahead. Suddenly my laugh broke into a sob and I felt my chest heaving and heaving. Ursula's did the same thing, and before we knew it, we were both crying and laughing at the same time.

It was crazy and it hurt a lot. Finally we stopped and I sprawled out on the floor and faced the

window. Ursula lay back with her head on my chest, looking out too. The night sky was lighting up with the approaching sun.

"Promise me one thing, Leon," she said. "Promise me we'll stay together."

"I promise," I said, and I stroked her hair. "And you know what else? We can take Pin home."

"Oh, no, Leon," she said and sat up quickly. "We can't. We shouldn't."

"Of course we can. He's the doctor's size. I'll bring over some of the doctor's clothes, dress him, and take him back."

"No, Leon. I don't want you to do that."

I stared at her in anger. It wasn't like Ursula to reject Pin. The thought of it brought a numbness into my legs and I had difficulty sitting up.

"Of course you want that, Ursula. How do you think Pin will feel all alone here until this office is sold and a new doctor comes. Perhaps he won't like the new doctor. Besides, Pin's always wanted to come home with us. It was the doctor who didn't permit it and the doctor's dead."

"But would that be wise? I mean, people might talk and . . ."

"People don't have to know our personal business. I won't live in that house without Pin. Make up your mind quickly. Otherwise you can go live with Uncle Hymie."

"Oh, no. I don't want to live with them."

"Well?"

"All right," she said, "but do it at night."

"Of course I'll do it at night. No one has to know our business. Don't worry," I said reaching out for her hand, "things'll be all right."

Ursula nodded slowly and leaned against me

again, her head on my chest. The sunlight got stronger and stronger. We remained there like that for quite a while. Ursula fell asleep and then woke up. Quietly we got up and left the office. We drove through the quiet, empty streets to home. When we got there, Ursula made us something to eat. She tried to keep the kitchen as clean as mother had wanted it. She tried for about ten minutes, and then she gave it up with a silly little laugh.

"Why am I wiping the inside of the garbage can lid? It's so stupid."

"You're not the little homemaker your mother was," I said, imitating Pin's tone of voice.

"I don't care. I can only do my best and my best is what any normal person would do."

"It's all right with me and I'm sure it'll be all right with Pin. The doctor never worried about it. In fact, he was oblivious to mother's antics."

Afterward, we went upstairs and dressed to meet our uncles and aunts. We were determined, right from the start, to impress them with our maturity and independence. We knew they weren't anxious to take on any new responsibilities, and our actions could help them rationalize not getting too involved.

The funeral was quick. People came from all over the area. Afterward, my uncles and aunts came home with us. My Aunt Dorothy was for discussing what would now happen to Ursula and me, but my Uncle Hymie had the sensitivity to put it off until the following night. Ursula and I sat together on the couch in the living room for a good part of the day. Of course, we ate very little. Some of the kids came, but it was mostly adults who visited. They spent their time talking to my uncles and aunts.

Along about eight o'clock the next night, my Uncle Hymie asked Ursula and me to step into the dining room with him. We sat around the table and he described our financial condition. He had done all the legal work, checking on the wills, bank accounts and investments. I was really surprised to hear just how well off we were. I knew father had a big practice, but I didn't know he had so many investments, good investments. Everything was left to us. I don't know whether or not this bothered Uncle Hymie. He had an inscrutable face when he discussed business. He was to Wall Street what my father was to medicine—coldly calculating.

"Leon," he said, "you're over eighteen now, and legally in control of a great amount of wealth. However, I . . . that is, none of us expect you to be able to handle it all by yourself."

"I don't see why not, Uncle Hymie."

"I don't think you fully comprehend yet just what is involved here."

"Yes, he does," Ursula said quickly. "Leon is very intelligent. He's brilliant."

"No one is saying he isn't, Ursula, but for a young man like Leon to be suddenly burdened with all this responsibility . . ."

"I don't mind responsibility," I said. "I used to help mother with her financial planning from time to time," I added. It was an out-and-out lie. Mother did little or no financial planning. Uncle Hymie sat back, looking a little disturbed. As far as I could see, there was little resemblance between him and my father. My father's face was lean, his features sharp. Uncle Hymie's face was round. He had a double chin and thick lips.

"Is that so?" he said. "Tell me, what do you plan to do with the shares of Sante Fe?" He was testing me just so I would feel inadequate.

"I'm going to hold them," I said quickly, looking directly at him. "They've gone up five points since we bought them, and father expected them to go to twelve during the coming year. You know what the exporting of all that grain is going to do?" I hardly knew what I was talking about, but Uncle Hymie was taken aback. He was floored by my confidence. "Anyway, I have a good legal and financial advisor in Mr. Orseck. Father trusted him, didn't he?"

"Well, yes, I suppose. . . . Look, Leon, your Aunt Dorothy thinks you two should come to live with her. You could come to live with us also. Maybe you could spend some time with both of us."

"We'll be fine here," I said quickly. I felt Ursula's hand touch mine under the table. I held her fingers.

"I could never leave this place without knowing you two were well taken care of. Why, your father and mother would expect that from us, to say the least."

"No, they wouldn't," Ursula said. "Father especially would want us to become independent. He brought us up that way."

"It's out of the question," he said.

"You've already stated, Uncle Hymie, that I'm eighteen and legally in control of my finances."

"Yes, but Ursula's just sixteen. She has to have a proper home."

"She'd have it here with me. This is her home. This is where she's going to school too. How can you pull her out of all that?"

"And what will she do when you go to college next

year? Live here by herself?" That question took me by surprise. I hadn't thought of it. Ursula's grip on my hand tightened.

"I'm not going to go to college," I said softly. "There's no reason to anymore."

"What? Why not?"

"As far as I can see, we're financially as comfortable as we need be."

"But there's more to life than being financially well-off, Leon. Look, there's no sense in our discussing it anymore. Even if I agreed, your Aunt Dorothy would insist. If you want to stay, Leon, there is nothing I can do. But Ursula will have to come and live with one of us."

"Then you'll have to go to court to make her," I said.

"That's damn right," Ursula added. Uncle Hymie just sat looking at us. Then he shook his head and stood up. "And even if you did win, you'd have to drag me to your house and keep me under constant guard day and night, because the first chance I got, I'd run back."

"I don't think either of you is thinking clearly," he said, and left. A moment later, Aunt Dorothy came in, and we went through a similar argument. Finally frustrated, she left too. Ursula and I went upstairs to our rooms. About an hour or so later, all of them came up. We gathered in Ursula's room. Uncle Hymie was their spokesman.

"We've decided to let you two have your way for a while, Leon. In a short time, I'm sure, as is everyone else, that you'll realize what's best for Ursula and yourself. At least, until she goes off to college." They all nodded. My Aunt Sadie looked as if she were about to cry.

68

"I'm not going to college either," Ursula said.

"You may change your mind," Aunt Dorothy responded. She pursed her lips and placed her hands on her hips.

"I doubt it," I said. They all stood there looking at us in silence for a few moments longer. Then they turned and left the room. In the morning all of them went home. We had breakfast together (Ursula insisted on preparing it just to show her abilities), and then we escorted them to the door. My Aunt Sadie cried as she kissed us. She was so high-strung and emotionally upset that Uncle Hymie had his hands full with her and paid us little attention at the end.

"You'll call us the moment you change your minds, right?" Aunt Dorothy said. I nodded, but Ursula wouldn't even grant her that much. "And we'll call you periodically." I nodded again. They finally left, each of them touching us on the arms and face. I closed the door. For a long moment, Ursula and I stood there alone in the big empty house.

"We did it," she said coming up to me and taking my arm in hers. "I never thought they'd leave us."

"They saw we meant business," I said. She laughed. Then we went into the living room and flopped on the couch. Simultaneously, we both had the same idea and jumped up to take off the plastic covers.

"We'll be all right, won't we, Leon?"

"Sure we will. No problems. I'll see Mr. Orseck tomorrow and plan out our financial life, just like I told Uncle Hymie. There's nothing to worry about."

"I knew you could handle it," she said. Her face was lit up with happiness. "They were like putty in

your hands. You are brilliant, Leon. You are. We will be all right."

"Certainly. And tonight we'll go and get Pin. We'll drive over to the office, dress him and put him in the backseat."

The smile left her face.

"Where will you keep him? I mean . . ."

"The room behind the garage. It'll be perfect. Don't you agree?" She nodded slowly.

"I feel like soaking in a hot bath. Will you come up in a while and wash my back?"

"Sure," I said. I watched her walk away. Since the abortion, we hadn't done anything as intimate as that. I sat there in that empty living room for about fifteen minutes before I got up to go upstairs. It was very lonely. I couldn't wait to get Pin over.

When I opened the door to the bathroom, I found Ursula sitting in the tub with her eyes closed. I walked over and looked down at her. Some foam from the suds had settled around the nipples of her breasts. She opened her eyes and looked up at me. She smiled and I knelt down to lift the warm washcloth out of the water. She sat up and leaned forward so I could rub her back. I waited as she reached back and held her hair away. Then I began, moving the cloth in small circular motions.

"How's that feel?"

"It feels good, Leon. Real good," she said. Then she leaned back again. Still kneeling beside the tub, I stared at her. She smiled again. "I'm not afraid anymore," she added. "Not afraid."

Chapter 5

EVEN THOUGH OUR UNCLES AND AUNTS CALLED LESS AND less frequently that first year, we sweated it out, expecting at any time for them to go to family court and get an order for Ursula to go live with them. Of course, they never did. Ursula believed it was probably because they really never wanted the responsibility and aggravation involved in acting as guardians. She said we got them off the hook by being so independent. Maybe she was right. Ursula would certainly have made life difficult for whomever she was forced to live with. They knew that.

When Ursula finally did turn eighteen, we had a great celebration. The three of us had a fantastic dinner and drank lots of champagne. Ursula got wiped out and I had to carry her upstairs to put her

to sleep. Afterward, Pin and I sat in the living room and talked quietly about her future. She continually refused to go to college. Pin thought I ought to try harder to talk her into it. I did try, but she was determined not to go. Finally she settled on the job at the library. I think she first did it just so we would stop bothering her about her future, but after a while, she got to like the job a lot. It paid little, but she didn't really need the money anyway. I guess it was a good way for her to occupy her day. She used to come home and tell us all about the people who came in and what books they requested.

"I like the whole atmosphere of quiet in there," she would say. "The serenity, the peacefulness of the place. It's very relaxing."

The library really didn't have that many books in it and there weren't that many people using it. Some kind of government funds supported it, I think. Ursula worked with an old lady, a Miss Spartacus, who lived with her sister. Ursula said Miss Spartacus was at least seventy-three years old. She had been with the library as far back as anyone could remember. In fact, she had become a librarian right out of high school. I used to kid her about that and tell her someday she'd be another Miss Spartacus. The old lady was a short woman with very thin hair. Ursula said she was close to being bald. Her nose and eyebrows twitched from a nervous condition. When I wanted to get a reaction out of Ursula, I would tell her to stop twitching her nose.

"Miss Spartacus has little gray hairs all over her face," Ursula told me. "She could shave in the morning."

"That's not really unusual for old women," Pin said.

Ursula said that Miss Spartacus went to the reserved book racks to eat lunch every day. She said she nibbled on her food like a squirrel.

"She even holds it like a squirrel. All she eats is nuts and fruits."

"You'll have to invite her to dinner one night," Pin said. I laughed.

Actually, we invited very few people to our house. Aside from an occasional salesman and some kids selling cookies or magazines, people rarely came to our door. The first year after mother and father died, I used to have kids over on weekends, but gradually they stopped coming and I stopped asking them. Ursula withdrew completely. I don't know how she finished her last year in high school. She was absent so much. I once asked Pin if he minded our lack of company.

"I suppose you were used to something entirely different over there in father's office. There were people coming and going all day long."

"It's a change, but it's not a bad change. I've grown to like our privacy," he said. "Besides, the only people who came over there were people with troubles of one sort or another. The more people you know, the more trouble you learn about."

I think he meant it, although sometimes I wondered if he wasn't just saying it for my benefit. He was right about people bringing their troubles, though. One afternoon, not long after the funeral, I brought Marcia Matterson home with me. Ursula was still in school and I thought it was a good opportunity to get a piece of what Marcia was so charitably giving out. The doctor had told us about nymphomaniacs, but I couldn't imagine one until I met Marcia. She had absolutely no concern about

whom she was with or how often she was with someone. Although she was heavy in the hips, she had a reasonably attractive face and very big breasts—enormous ones, in fact. I had a secret desire to weigh one, betting with myself that they weighed at least ten pounds apiece. I gave her a highball, although it really wasn't necessary to pump her full of booze first. She was quite prepared to hop right into bed with me.

Pin was sitting in the corner of the living room in the shadows. He liked sitting in the shadows because he said it put him in a pensive mood. Sometimes I would sit in the opposite corner in the shadows and think too. I didn't introduce Marcia to him when we first came in. I really didn't think he wanted to meet her anyhow. Pin was really a little prudish when I think about it. He could also be very bashful and clam right up. That would get very embarrassing and uncomfortable for all present.

So Marcia and I went upstairs to my room. She drank her drink very quickly and we embraced on my bed. We were fully clothed and for the first ten or fifteen minutes, I just squeezed her breasts and kissed her neck. I really wasn't convinced myself that I was going to have intercourse. (I really wanted to say screw or fuck, but the doctor's influence lasted long after his death.) In any case, though, she was positive about what she wanted. She grew very impatient with me and undressed herself. I sat there watching her struggle to get that sweater over her head. Her breasts, freed of the bra, fell with relief onto her. I leaned forward and gently lifted one with the palm of my right hand. I bounced it softly, as if weighing it. She smiled and moaned and pursed her lips.

Somehow she turned me off. I don't really know why I suddenly felt that way. Perhaps I was just turned off by her gross body. For the first time, I noticed that there were little dark hairs growing over her lower lip. That bothered me, I know. She unzipped her skirt and then looked at me in anticipation. I was just sitting there, staring blankly at her naked bosom.

"Well?"

"Shh," I said. "I think I heard Pin."

"Who?"

"Pin. He's downstairs. He didn't see us come in."

"Who's Pin?"

"He lives with us. Shh." She sat there, completely quiet, with this most serious and at the same time puzzled expression on her face. After a few more moments, she spoke.

"I don't hear anything."

"I did."

"So what? Go lock your door."

"I don't have a lock on it."

"Well, he wouldn't just walk in on you, would he?"

"He has in the past," I lied. She was getting very impatient and very angry now. She crossed her arms over her bosom as if she had just realized she was naked.

"Look," she said, "are you going to or aren't you?"

"I think not," I said. "Thanks anyway," I added. She was dumbfounded. Her mouth dropped and she gave me a look of amazement.

"What the fuck . . ."

"I'm sorry, but I really do appreciate your coming over. Really, I do."

"What are you, nuts or somethin' . . . ?"

"I'll let you get dressed now," I said, and I got up and walked out of the room and down to the living room.

"Who's upstairs, Leon?" Pin asked.

"Some slut. I know what you're going to say, but you don't have to say it. I changed my mind about her. We didn't do a thing."

"Getting sensible in your old age, huh?"

"Yeah. Who the hell knows what she's got by now? Everybody's been putting it to her."

"I'm glad you thought of that. I'd hate to have to give you penicillin shots."

"I know what you mean," I said. Just then, Marcia appeared, fully dressed again.

"Who are you talking to?"

"Pin."

"Who?" She struggled to see into the shadows. He was really back in the corner. "Why don't you put on a light in here?"

"He likes it this way," I said. She stepped a little closer.

I suppose Pin's appearance could be a bit frightening to someone who first saw him. He sat so stiffly in his chair and stared so directly ahead of him. We had given Pin some of father's best suits to wear. He was dressed in a nice tweed at the time. Marcia took a few more steps into the living room. The little light coming in from the windows threw a glow over Pin's face. When that happened, he became sort of transparent to someone first seeing him. Of course, Ursula and I were always used to it, but someone first seeing him would be attracted by that transparency. He would see right into Pin's head, right through the skull, see the nasal passages, the teeth

and gums, the inner ears, the nerves of the eyes leading to the brain. Oh, yes, he would see the brain.

Anyhow, Marcia's reaction was typical. She gasped, put her fist into her mouth, turned and ran out of the room. When she got to the front door, she turned around again and gave me the funniest look, a mixture of shock and pity. Then she rushed out and slammed the door behind her. I had to laugh. The nerve of her, a pitiful creature like that, giving me a look of pity.

"Not a very emotionally stable young lady," Pin said.

"To say the least. She's a regular nympho," I added and walked up to him to pull him and his chair out of the shadows. "Sorry about the way she reacted. I was about to introduce you to her."

"No loss as far as I can see."

"I know. I guess I was just a little curious. I won't be doing that again."

"Maybe you should get out more, though, mix with people your own age."

"Naw, I'll be all right. Really. It was just a whim. It's OK," I said. Then Ursula came home. I didn't mention Marcia. As far as I was concerned, the whole affair had ended.

So I guess it's pretty safe to say we lived cloistered lives for a long time after the death of my mother and father. A lot of boys wanted to go out with Ursula, but she didn't have the interest. I had a few dates now and then, but a great deal of my time was taken up running the house and father's investments. Once a week I would go to see Mr. Orseck and go over the finances. We were doing very, very well, and I had him send a copy of our assets to

Uncle Hymie just to prove to him that I could handle things better than he could. I guess he didn't like knowing that, because he never responded.

From time to time Ursula and I would go out to a movie or take a long drive on a weekend afternoon. Once we even took Pin to the drive-in theater in Rock Hill, but he didn't enjoy sitting in the car. As a rule, he didn't enjoy riding in the car either. The three of us watched a lot of television, always discussing the programs at length. And I had my epic poem to work on. I wanted to do something modern, look for up-to-date dragons and monsters. The fear of the darkness was always the same throughout time, as far as I could see. Sometimes, I would look out of my window or the window of the living room and stare up at the night sky. There were no streetlights near our home. We were too far from the village. The darkness was deep and thick. At times like that, I could imagine the house to be a cave. I would write my best lines. When I read them to Pin, he knew immediately what I had been doing.

"You were thinking at the window again, huh?"

"Yes. I could feel Them out there, waiting for us to venture into Their darkness."

"You didn't see anything? I mean, actually?"

"No, not exactly. But it's just that setting, that unseen danger, that looms and affects my hero. He senses a mystical depth, an emptiness, and it all helps to form his personality, make him the man he is in the poem. He goes forward to face the challenge that They put forth."

"I see. Interesting," he said.

Ursula was always frightened by my talk of Them, the unknown monsters and dragons in our modern world. Or at least she liked to pretend she was

frightened like a little girl and curl up in bed under the covers and sob in the dark. Sometimes, after I read a passage or two of my poem that dealt with the darkness without, she'd run upstairs and do it. Pin had more patience with her at these times than I did.

"Ursula is a very sensitive and emotionally wounded person," he'd say. He knew how annoyed I got.

"But why does she have to go through this stupid charade all the time? It's just an attention-getter, that's all it is. I know it and she knows I know it."

"Nevertheless, Leon, you're the only one who can presently give her the affection she needs. You've got to humor her, play along."

"But just when I'm getting to a good part in my poem, just when I think I've hit some effective metaphors . . ."

"There'll be time for that. Go up to her."

"Aw, shit."

"You want me to go up to her?" he'd ask. I'd laugh at that.

"OK, OK, I'm going. I'm going. But don't go to sleep. I'll be back."

"It's all right. I'm not a bit tired tonight. I'll be here wide-awake when you return," he'd say, and I'd go upstairs to Ursula.

She'd be lying there in the darkness, under the covers in her bed, sobbing softly. I'd tiptoe into her room and stand by her bedside for a while. I knew she knew I was there, but she would just ignore me and continue to sob. So I'd kneel down and begin stroking her hair and whispering.

"It's all right, Ursula. It's all right. I'm here. It's all right."

She wouldn't respond. She'd just sob a little

softer. In the end, I'd have to crawl in beside her and hold her to me until she would fall asleep. When she did, I'd get up softly and tiptoe out of the room and go back down to Pin. He was there, waiting, but it was no good because I was usually too tired from putting Ursula to sleep.

"I'll just have a drink with you. I'll read some more some other night."

"Whatever."

"Do you think Ursula's getting worse?"

"Worse? In what sense, worse?"

"I mean, emotionally weaker instead of stronger and more mature?"

"I don't think she's worse. But I don't think she's much stronger, either."

"It wouldn't take much to shatter her, would it?" I asked. I felt a half smile on my face. It surprised me.

"Why would you want to?"

"I just wondered, that's all. It wouldn't take much to send her reeling into insanity."

"I suppose not. I don't see why you even want to think about it, though."

"It's just a thought that passed through my mind. That's all."

"Beware," he said. "Beware of yourself. There are forces in you, forces you're not familiar with, forces you may never understand."

I laughed. Pin could get downright serious and heavy at times. I teased him about it and told him it was father's influence on him. I didn't like being made to think deeply about myself like that. There was something frightening about it. When I stepped up to father's coffin in the funeral parlor that day, I had touched his hand because I had this overwhelming desire to know what it was like to touch someone

dead. I fought the desire, but it was stronger than me. He felt like Pin. I never told Pin that because I didn't want Pin to know he was right—I *was* at the mercy of forces I couldn't understand at times. Of course, Ursula saw me do it. She was standing right at my side. I felt her staring. She asked me about it much later on.

We were lying together in the dark. I thought she was asleep. Suddenly she just asked me why I had done it and what it felt like. I told her and she was quiet for a long time afterward. I thought she had fallen asleep. Then I suddenly felt her fingers touch my hand, right below the knuckles. I wasn't expecting it and I jumped from the surprise and shock. She laughed and I got very mad, but in the end, I laughed too.

We were a lot alike, Ursula and I, remarkably alike. Often we had the same thoughts at the same time. I used to think we could merge and become a new creature: a kind of man-woman who could turn into itself to experience a wild but total ecstasy. I was very satisfied with our relationship and our way of life. It seemed to me that the three of us had a perfect world.

That's why I resented it so much when she brought Stanley into it.

Chapter 6

THE FIRST TIME URSULA MENTIONED STANLEY Friedman, I knew that it was more than a casual acquaintance. There was a sparkle in her eyes, an excitement in her face that was there only on special occasions, moments of great happiness and satisfaction. She spoke very fast, hardly able to contain the excitement. Her restraint was visible. She waited anxiously for my questions and comments so that she could continue to describe and talk about him. Pin seemed very happy for her. He listened with deliberate great interest. This caused her to direct a lot of what she said toward him.

"There is this boy," she began, "young man, I should say, who's been coming to the library every day this past week."

"Must be quite a reader."

"He is, he is, but I think he's also coming to see me."

"What makes you say that?"

"I'll look up from my work occasionally and always catch him staring at me."

"Do you stare back?"

"He's very nice-looking. He's got a wooden leg, though."

"A wooden leg?"

"A wooden leg!" Pin said. He perked up at that.

"Well, actually, it's only wooden from below the knee down. He's a Vietnam veteran."

"Oh," Pin said. I thought he sounded disappointed.

"Does he use crutches?" I asked.

"No, he seems to be able to get around pretty well without them. He limps, of course."

"You know his name, don't you?"

"Certainly. He's got a library card. His name's Stanley Friedman."

"Stanley Friedman? I don't recall that name."

"He just recently moved here. Came with his mother. His father's dead. His mother's pretty sick, though. They live with Tillie Kratner, between Woodridge and Mountaindale."

"Is that so?" I wanted to change the topic, but Ursula was determined to go on about him.

"Yes. She's his mother's sister. His mother's got some kind of a lung condition. He's a nice boy, very polite."

"Young man, you mean."

"Yes," she said smiling. She didn't pay any attention to my sarcasm. "He doesn't talk much,

kind of inhibited, I think. Maybe the war experience did that to him."

"You seem to know a great deal about him."

"That's only from prying with my questions. That little bit of information is a week's worth of questions, believe it or not."

"No wonder he stares at you. You've been showing him a great deal of attention."

"Oh, I have not. Not any more than anyone would. He doesn't have any wrong ideas about me."

"What does Miss Spartacus think of him?"

"She hasn't really met him."

"I thought so. He deliberately comes to you."

"Oh, Leon, you're such a little detective," she said, and waltzed upstairs. Pin laughed, but I didn't think it was all that funny.

Every day after that, Ursula came home with one story or another about Stanley Friedman. She said he was reading a lot of religious books, concentrating on the Far Eastern religions. Gradually, I got a full physical description of him. She made him sound like Errol Flynn or somebody. I was sure she was exaggerating. According to her, he had long, wavy, light brown hair, very soft looking, blue-green eyes that kept a continual dancing smile on his face, a sharp, straight nose and a strong mouth. His complexion was dark and he was at least six feet tall. From the way she talked about his teeth, you'd have thought he advertised toothpaste.

"He gives the impression of great strength. Very broad shouldered, long, powerful-looking forearms and a tight, slim waist."

"Sounds like Vic Tanny."

"If it weren't for that limp . . ."

"Did he describe his war wound to you and how he got it? I'm sure you must've asked him."

"He stepped on a mine. It blew his lower leg off right then and there. It's amazing he didn't bleed to death."

"Amazing." I looked at Pin and smiled.

"But with this modern war, he says a lot of guys were saved who would have died in World War Two or even Korea."

"Incredible. Isn't it wonderful, Pin?" He pretended not to have heard my sarcasm. Ursula was finally beginning to get annoyed, though. I could see it in her face, the way she tried to hold it together stiffly.

"He's originally from the Bronx."

"Is he? How's his dying mother?"

"Not so good. They thought the air up here would help her, but it hasn't done much. He says she has a degenerating condition."

"Tell me," I said, leaning over toward her, "with all this conversation going on, how does he get time to read?"

"We don't really talk that much. I admit, we talk more than we did at first, but not very much. Miss Spartacus frowns upon long conversations in the library."

"Good for Miss Spartacus," I said, and I got up and went upstairs to write.

Finally one night she didn't come home right after work. In fact, Pin and I had supper alone. I was very worried because she hadn't done anything like that for the longest time. Pin sat there very coolly. He knew all the time. I admired his insight. I mean, the thought passed through my mind, but only for an

instant. He was obviously convinced. It was almost as if he could read someone's future. He knew the inevitability of what was to come. Stoic, inscrutable Pin.

"I wonder if I should keep all this stuff hot for Ursula," I said, testing him.

"I don't think so. She'll have eaten somewhere when she gets home."

"I hope she had enough money with her to pay for the food," I said, continuing to tease out responses from him. "She's so absentminded about money. She hardly ever takes anything but some small change along with her when she goes to work."

"She won't need any. Someone will pay for her."

"She won't like that. Ursula doesn't like strangers doing things for her."

"It won't be a stranger."

"You bastard," I said, raising my voice. "Why don't you just come out and say it—say it."

"What?"

"Ursula's gone somewhere with that crippled soldier with the dying mother."

"So?"

"She could have called me and said she wasn't coming home for supper. She could have done that, couldn't she? She knew we'd be waiting for her."

"Must've been a spur-of-the-moment deal. What's the difference? There's no real harm done, is there?"

"I would have prepared less."

"Big deal."

"You're always defending her. Always." He didn't say anything further. I began to feel stupid for getting so excited and obviously emotional over Ursula's actions, so I dropped the topic and finished

eating. Afterward, Pin and I went into the living room and did some reading. Along about nine or nine-thirty, I heard a car drive up and a door slam. A moment later, Ursula entered. I had made up my mind to act very nonchalant and unconcerned about where she had been and what she had done.

"Hi," she said, coming into the living room.

"Hi," I said dryly. I looked back at my book immediately. She walked right over to Pin, ignoring my lack of interest. It was her way of getting me to listen to something when she knew that I wasn't particularly keen on it.

"Oh, Pin," she said, "Pin, I had the most wonderful time, the best time I've had these past few years." She squeezed herself and turned around like a dumb schoolgirl. I had to respond.

"Figured you were having a good time somewhere," I said.

"Oh, I did. We went out to eat, took a long ride all the way to Port Jervis and ate in a restaurant by the water. He talked and talked. He's so interesting," she said, turning completely back to me again. "He's seen so much and he's a very sensitive person. I mean," she said sitting on the hassock right by Pin, "he hasn't just lived through events, he's reacted to them and been affected by them."

"We still don't know whom you are talking about," I said, looking down into the book. I wasn't reading anything, though. All the words were a blur.

"Oh, yes, that's right." She laughed. "How stupid of me. I'm talking about Stan."

"Stan?"

"You know, Stanley Friedman."

"The boy with the leg blown off."

"Yes," she answered, closing her eyes and open-

ing them. "But when you're with him, you don't think of that."

"Well, I don't see how you would, unless you were down there washing his feet," I said, laughing. Pin didn't laugh. Ursula looked at me for a moment and then turned back to Pin.

"It was horrible, Pin. The killing he saw, the women and children he says he saw burned and maimed. It was horrible just to hear about it."

"How many did he kill?" I asked. She didn't turn around.

"He killed people, but he said he never knowingly shot a woman or child."

"Sure."

"He cracked up from what he saw," she went on, speaking very quickly. "They had to send him to a hospital because he had a nervous breakdown. He said he came to a village that had been hit by napalm and there were these children still being held in the arms of their mothers. . . . He couldn't even describe it."

"He's probably bulling you."

"No, I believe him."

"I thought he stepped on a mine."

"He did," she said turning sharply. "After they sent him back to the fighting."

"So now he spends his time sitting in a library reading about Far Eastern religions?"

"He's looking for an answer, a reason. He says he wants to dedicate himself to understanding what it is in us that makes us do the things we do."

"That's not very flattering."

"What isn't? What are you talking about now?"

"Dedicating himself to that and then taking you out to dinner."

"Leon, sometimes you talk like an idiot, you know," she said, and she stood up. "I don't know why you're being so nasty. I don't, I really don't," she said, her voice getting very high-pitched. Then she started to cry and ran out of the room and upstairs.

"Jesus," I said.

"She's right, you know," Pin said.

"What right? What?"

"You've been pretty unpleasant to her, Leon."

"I was just teasing her a bit."

"Yeah, but you see how happy she is, how seriously she takes it all. Why don't you apologize to her. She's really the happiest I've seen her since your parents died."

"Apologize! For what?" He didn't say anything. "Oh, damn. All right," I said getting up. "I'll go up and wipe her little tears away."

As I walked up the stairs, I felt my hand grow numb again. The feeling crept up my fingers, over my knuckles and to my wrist. I held my arm up and let the hand dangle for a moment. It was puzzling, but not painful. Ursula was sprawled across her bed crying. For a moment I just stood there looking in. I had a confusing reaction. First I enjoyed her unhappiness, but then I felt sorry for her and lousy that I had caused her to be unhappy. So I walked in and sat next to her on the bed.

"OK," I said. "I'm sorry. I was just having a little fun."

"You . . . you've been doing this to me ever since I told you about Stanley. I tried to ignore it, hoping you would stop."

"I have not."

"Yes, you have. You have, Leon," she said,

wiping her eyes and sitting up on her elbow. "I've been paying attention to you. I don't know why you've been doing it. You don't even know him. You haven't even met him, yet you act as though you hate him."

"That's ridiculous. If I haven't met him, I couldn't deliberately not like him, could I? You're overreacting. I've just been having fun with you, that's all. Come on," I said, stroking her hair, "I said I was sorry."

"It's just that he's the first interesting person I've met in that place since I've been there."

"Sure."

"And I enjoy his company and I find him pleasant. There's nothing phony about him."

"All right."

"You will, too, Leon."

"Maybe I will."

"Then you want to meet him?"

"What'dya mean?"

"I mean, could I have him over one night, maybe for dinner?"

"Sure," I said. "Why not?"

"Because I told him all about you," she said, smiling now, "and he says I have a brother complex because I brag so much about you."

"I bet."

"No, really." She paused for a moment and looked down. "I even told him about Pin," she added.

"You did?"

"Uh-huh."

"What did he say then?"

"He wants to meet him too." She looked up at me quickly.

"Good," I said. I wanted him to meet Pin. I wanted her to bring him home and introduce him to Pin. That would be something. I had seen the effect Pin had on people who first met him. It wouldn't take long for this guy to understand that Pin wasn't the kind of person you could snow over. Pin always saw through false people. Phonies who stood before him immediately felt naked and exposed. They became speechless and confused. I was convinced that this guy was probably three-quarters hot air. He must've seen that Ursula was very impressionable and gone right to it. But it would be a different story when he confronted Pin. I couldn't wait.

"Sure," I said. "Why don't you bring him around this Saturday night? That'll give you a chance to whip up a roast, a real dinner. I'll go get some good wine. Pin loves to sit around sipping good wine before dinner and talking to people."

"That sounds great, Leon. I just knew you'd want to meet him."

"I do, I do. And Pin does too. I know he does because after you described him to us, he said I'd like to meet that guy. He sounds like a terrific person."

She got up and went to the bathroom to wash her face. Her makeup had spread from the tears and made streaks down her cheeks. I told her it looked like war paint and she laughed. I watched her for a while. She talked while she undressed. I heard all about her meal and the different topics that she and Stan had discussed going and coming back from Port Jervis. She said that Stanley was having a hard time readjusting. In a way, she said, he was drifting.

"He's trying to find himself again, and I'd like to

help him as much as I can." She stepped out of her skirt and unfastened her bra.

"Yeah, that's nice. Now what are you doing?"

"I'm going to take a shower and relax. I'll be down in a while and watch some television with you and Pin."

"OK," I said. She stepped behind the glass doors of the shower stall and turned on the water. I watched her moving behind the glazed window. Her body took on a distorted, impressionistic fluidity because of the design in the glass.

I remained there for a while and watched. It had a wild effect on me. I got dizzy and had to sit down for a moment. Ursula was singing. She seemed happier than I had seen her for a long while. For some reason, that annoyed me, and finally, I left because of a growing feeling of antagonism for her. When I got downstairs, I didn't say anything to Pin for a while. He got impatient.

"Well?"

"She's all right. She's fine. She's terrific, in fact."

"So why are you so uptight?"

"Who's uptight?"

"Come off it, Leon. I know when you're uptight."

"Oh, Jesus," I said, "do I have to put up with everybody's little temperament? I'm not uptight, damnit."

"Forget I said anything."

"I'm sorry," I said. I walked over and stood beside him. "I have so many conflicting feelings going through me sometimes. You know," I added in almost a whisper, "sometimes I feel as if I could commit great violence, even murder."

He didn't say anything. It grew so quiet we could hear Ursula upstairs. She was still singing.

Chapter 7

PIN AND I SAT IN THE LIVING ROOM WAITING. URSULA WAS in the kitchen cooking. The dining room was all set up. It was half past six. Because of daylight savings time, it had been dark since five o'clock. There had been another heavy snow, but the roads were well plowed and the world outside looked like a jeweled kingdom. Passing clouds turned the moonlight on and off, making the branches of trees flicker and sparkle. Because we had no television on, no radio, nor any music, we could hear the clatter of dishes and silverware coming from the kitchen. Pin was very quiet. Lately he always reacted that way just before he knew he was going to meet someone new. In the old days, when he was with my father in the office, he could strike up a conversation with a

complete stranger so quickly and so smoothly that it would be difficult for an observer to realize that it was a complete stranger. Now, living in the cloistered world with us, he had grown out of touch with things. I could see the nervousness in his face. He was dressed in one of father's double-breasted suits because he favored them. Actually, he reminded me a little bit of the doctor, sitting there so rigidly in his chair.

More and more Pin had been striking up memories of my father for me. It had gotten to the point where I was confusing the two faces in my mind. He used all of the doctor's favorite expressions and dressed in his clothes . . . well, it was just getting more and more difficult to distinguish the two in my mind. I sat there wondering how the doctor would react to Ursula's bringing a man home for dinner. Would he be cordial? Formal?

At a quarter to seven, the doorbell rang. Stanley was fifteen minutes early. Ursula came out to the living room, wiping her hands on her apron. Pin didn't move. I bit my lower lip gently and waited to see what Ursula would do next. I was waiting for her to ask me to let him in. I knew it would come to that. I would have to introduce him to Pin. In the end, she wouldn't have the nerve. I smiled to myself and stood up. The doorbell rang again.

"I suppose that's our little soldier boy."

"He's early. Probably anxious to meet you and Pin. You let him in, OK, Leon?"

"Sure. Go back into the kitchen, Ursula. Get the meal going. I'm starved."

"Thanks, Leon."

"You ready?" I said to Pin.

"Of course I'm ready. What's the big deal?"

"No big deal," I said. I walked to the door, hesitated, and then opened it with a rough jerk. Stanley Friedman, carrying a box of candy wrapped in holiday packaging, stood smiling in at me. He was much stouter than I had imagined, but he was a good-looking guy. He did have wavy, light brown hair and a nice smile. It was a wide smile, warm and seemingly quite sincere. When he did step in, I saw that he was about an inch taller than me.

"Hi. I'm Leon."

"Stan," he said extending his hand. "I've heard a great deal about you." He stepped in. "Ursula thinks a lot of you."

"I think a lot of her."

"Well," he said, holding out the candy, "I brought some assorted chocolates. Hope you people go for them."

"Pin loves them," I said. "You can hang your coat up right here." I opened the hall closet and checked out his right leg as he slipped out of his coat. It was difficult, if not impossible, to tell it was partly wooden. He limped some as we started down the corridor, though.

"This is quite a house, deceptive from outside," he said, turning to me just as we reached the doorway of the living room. I noticed he had a slight lisp. For a guy who was supposed to be somewhat introverted, he seemed pretty relaxed. That introverted stuff was probably phony, I thought.

"Yes. It's an old house, but a comfortable one. My father, the doctor, did a lot to modernize it while he was alive. I'm afraid Ursula and I don't do much for it now, except see that it's kept reasonably clean."

"It's nice. Ursula's hard at work, I suppose."

"She's going to show off her domestic talents."

"She told me you were quite a cook too."

"I've had plenty of practice. Pin, too, is a great cook," I added. "He knows quite a few recipes. He's quite the gourmet."

"Can't wait to meet him," he said, and I noticed the first signs of nervousness in his face.

"He's right in there," I said, indicating the living room. My heart began beating fast, just as it always did right before someone new met Pin. I moved a little faster than Stan did because I wanted to be standing beside Pin when they met. I wanted to see the expression on Stan's face. "Right over in the corner in that chair."

"Right," he said, moving across the room. The limp became more pronounced. As we approached, I flicked on the little lamp just to the right of Pin. His face came alive.

"Pin," I said, "this is Ursula's friend Stan. Stan, this is our lifelong friend and companion, Pin," I added, and turned quickly to see Stan's face. He smiled and shot a glance at me. I must've looked very serious because his face snapped into a serious expression. There was a moment of silence during which Stan's face seemed to tighten and then relax. He straightened up as if he were being presented to one of his old officers and then shot his hand out so fast it took me by surprise. I stepped back.

"It's a pleasure to meet you, sir," he said. Pin was surprised too. He didn't even lift his hand to shake. But Stan thrust his out so fast and so hard that he was only inches away. Then he had the nerve, the audacity, to push his hand into Pin's. Naturally, Pin,

being the gentleman he is, shook and disregarded Stan's aggressiveness. "I have heard a great deal about you, a great deal." When he let go, Pin's hand dropped to his lap. I stood looking at Stanley and feeling a great sense of disappointment and anger settle over me. His reaction to Pin was a letdown. He was at ease with him, almost as much at ease as Ursula and I were. He was as nonchalant as could be. I watched him back up a few steps and look around the room. "Very nice, big room. You don't see many houses with these tall ceilings anymore."

"Pin," I said, keeping my eyes on Stanley as I talked, "Stan has brought some assorted chocolates. After dinner, we can come in and have a few."

Stanley turned and smiled. Then he limped to one of the big chairs and settled himself in it. I was fascinated with his poise. Pin eyed the chocolates greedily. It made me laugh.

"He'd like to skip dinner and have them now, wouldn't you, Pin?"

"I can wait, Leon. I have a great deal of self-control."

"We can't permit that," Stanley said. Then he leaned over toward us. "We can't do anything to spoil Ursula's dinner, now, can we? For a woman, a dinner is like a performance," he said, sitting back again. He was right at home.

"She oughta perform more often then," I said. It was a bit cruel and I regretted saying it immediately. "But I'm sure she'll do well."

"Ursula tells me that you're working on an epic poem."

"She did?" I wasn't sure whether I felt indignant or proud.

"I'd like to read some of it sometime."

"Maybe Leon'll read some of it after dinner," Pin said.

"Yes. Perhaps, if we're all in the mood, I will read a little of it after dinner."

"I've always wanted to sit down and write something, but I've just lacked the patience. I admire you for having the discipline."

"Yes, it takes discipline. It's far from finished and it has a lot of rough spots."

"Don't be so modest, Leon," Pin said. "You know you've worked some of those lines over twenty or thirty times."

"I bet Pin's a good listener," Stanley said. His tone of voice was confusing. Was he mocking me or did he mean it?

"He's a good critic, very honest."

"I just say what I like and what I don't."

"Hi," Ursula said stepping into the room. Stanley got up. Standing from a sitting position was an awkward movement for him, but he didn't seem at all self-conscious about it. "I see you've gotten to meet everyone all right."

"From the way you described them, I feel as if I've known them almost as long as I've known you." They both laughed. I didn't like the way they looked at each other—how they tolerated the small silences between them and stared. I looked at Pin and smirked, but he seemed quite taken with Stanley. I was very surprised and somewhat annoyed.

"Care for a cocktail before dinner?" Ursula asked.
"Sure."

"I'll make them," I said. "What'll you have?"

"Bourbon and soda?"

"Sure thing. Pin, the usual?"

"Yes, Leon, the usual."

"What's his usual?"

"Ask him," I said quickly. Ursula's smile faded slowly, but Stanley's froze.

"Of course," he said, "how rude of me." He turned to Pin, shot a quick glance at Ursula, and then asked.

"I like a little rye, ginger ale and a slice of orange."

"Do you have the orange for his drink?" Ursula asked.

"Yes, I was prepared, sister dear," I said.

"You've got quite a house here," Stan said, and they got right into a conversation about the place. I made the drinks and distributed them. I never saw Pin so quiet. He just sat back and listened to Stan and Ursula talk. They were so involved in each other that I felt Pin and I should start our own conversation.

"You must tell us about the war," I said suddenly, interrupting them. Stan turned with a quizzical expression on his face, almost as if he were going to say, "What war?"

"I don't like talking about it too much. It was a horrible war."

"What war isn't?" Pin said.

"Hear, hear," I added and toasted the air and then drank.

"For us, it was militarily, politically and morally a big mistake," Stan added.

"You must be very bitter, then," I said, "having made a physical sacrifice for a big mistake."

"Well," he said, smiling that wide, warm smile, "I used to feel self-pity. That turned to anger. But now I've kind of settled into a warm indifference. A lot of suffering can have that effect on you."

"Very true," Pin said, "very true." I shot a glance at him. Did he have to be so impressed?

"I'm hungry," I said. I was getting impatient. Pin was a doting idiot, a great disappointment. Usually, he tore a newcomer apart, mocked him, ripped every remark down to its barest inanity. I rationalized and figured his new behavior was due to the fact that it had been so long since we had any guests.

"Everything's ready. Should we go into the dining room?"

"Good," I said. Stan stood up, still smiling. I was waiting for this moment too. Slowly I walked over to the corner and pulled the folded wheelchair out from behind the bookcase, figuring the sight of it would bring some unhappy memories back to Stan. I snapped it open and pushed it over to Pin, eyeing Stanley the whole time. He watched with great interest.

"Need any help?" he said. I was surprised by the offer.

"No," I said quickly and quite definitively. His smile left his face, but he stared with continued interest as I lifted Pin out of his seat and into the wheelchair. I set his feet comfortably in the footrests and stood up. Ursula had gone into the kitchen. Stanley waited.

"I almost ended up in one of those," he said. "I can appreciate the difficulties." His calmness amazed me. Nothing bothered him.

"No difficulties. We're quite used to things by now."

"Speak for yourself," Pin said. I pushed him forward and the three of us entered the dining room.

Chapter 8

DINNER LEFT ME IN A GREAT DEPRESSION. THE FOOD WAS good, but I hardly ate. What's more, Ursula didn't seem to care. She saw all the food left over, but she didn't mention it. Pin didn't touch very much of his food either. Stan was as charming and as relaxed as a person could be and Pin just sat there like a dumb one and soaked him up. I kicked him in the leg under the table a few times, but he didn't seem to feel it. He was too absorbed in Stan's conversation. I guess I'd have to admit that Stan was a witty guy at the table. He seemed to really enjoy our company. He knew just how to deliver a compliment, and he made Ursula feel like a million bucks. A rosiness came into her cheeks and her eyes sparkled with happiness. They laughed, ate off of each other's forks and

generally acted like two lovesick kids. I was polite and friendly, but not overly exuberant.

No matter what I said to try to throw him off rhythm and make him feel uncomfortable, Stan took it calmly. It was almost as if he expected it of me. Nothing Pin did surprised him either. Any other person would have felt self-conscious about Pin's staring, but he didn't. I caught him looking at Pin a few times, but he wasn't disturbed. He acted as though he had eaten a hundred meals with us. I began to wonder if Ursula had not prepared him in a way. It was a thought that angered me, because in effect that would mean that she conspired against us, Pin and myself.

"I understand your mother is dying," I said. They were giggling like kids on a merry-go-round. Ursula stopped and looked at me with a smile still on her face. He turned serious and straightened up in the seat. There was a moment's pause. I shot a quick glance at Pin, but he didn't seem to be sharing my satisfaction.

"Yes, she is in a bad way," he said, very matter-of-factly, I thought. "She's been struggling for health for some time now. It seems hopeless." Ursula stopped smiling. The heavy note I had set brought the result I was after.

"The country air hasn't helped then?"

"Not really, no."

"That's too bad," Pin said. He said it rather low.

"Unfortunate," I added. "Do you think you might leave the area then?"

"No. We're going to stay. For better or for worse, we're going to stay." Ursula looked relieved. I played with my fork for a moment and then looked at Pin.

"I think," I said, "Pin and I will go back to the living room now. You're about finished, aren't you, Pin?"

"Yes."

"Stan promised to help me with the dishes, didn't you, Stan?" Ursula teased.

"If I didn't, I guess I had better," he said. They giggled again. I couldn't stand it much longer, so I got up abruptly and pushed Pin away from the table. We went back into the living room and I made a fire. From the way Pin just sat there watching me, I knew that he sensed my uneasiness.

"You're pretty damn quiet tonight," I told him. "What do you really think of this guy? Is he all Ursula thinks he is?"

"I can't help liking him. You have to admit he's got a lot of personality."

"I didn't say he didn't have personality, and I didn't exactly say I didn't like him, did I?"

"You're trying not to like him, though, aren't you, Leon? Admit it to me and yourself."

"I just don't trust people until I get to know them better, that's all. I have the gut feeling that there's something more here than meets the eye. It's hard to put my finger on it."

"You've got your father's cynicism, that's all."

"Maybe so," I said. We sat quietly for a while. I passed him some of the chocolates and ate some myself. Then I made us after-dinner drinks and we sat listening to Ursula and Stan giggling in the kitchen. Occasionally their voices would die down and everything would become completely still. I imagined that they were kissing then.

"This is really the first man Ursula's been with since she had the abortion, isn't it?" Pin said.

"Yes. I suppose it's a good thing."

"Reluctantly, you do," Pin said. I had to laugh.

"Maybe I'm just acting like a big, dumb, overprotective brother."

"Maybe you're just acting like a jealous lover," Pin said. I was about to reply when they came into the living room.

"Care for an after-dinner drink?" I said. I made one for both of them. Then Ursula said that Stan would like to hear some of my poem.

"I really would," he said. We were all sitting around the fire drinking. I was in the mood, so I went upstairs and got the most recent two stanzas.

"This was just completed last night," I began. Pin looked pleased that I had chosen to read those.

"Oh, good," Ursula said, moving closer to Stan on the couch. "I didn't hear them yet."

"I suppose I should preface this by telling you that my hero, Testes, a sort of modern day Beowulf, is out to gain immortality by creating as much progeny as he can. He'll make love to anything female in the hopes of impregnating her. At this point, he's fathered one-hundred-and-seventy-three children."

"Quite a potent guy," Stan said, looking from me to Ursula.

"Yes, he damn well is," I said. "In these lines, he's contemplating rape for the first time."

"Oh, Leon," Ursula said, "why?"

"He's grown impatient with the courting process. It's too time consuming." I paused for a moment to be sure she wasn't going to interrupt me anymore and then began.

Gentle cloth night wrapped her bosom in luminous clinging moon. Testes watched from

the alley darkness. She moved through shadows, unaware that his loins were singing. The seed within him grew impatient to be planted in the fertile soil of her womb.

"That's one stanza," I said. Stan's eyes were big. He looked genuinely involved. Ursula was looking sad.

"Please go on," Stan said.

The shadows touched her face so that he could not read the lines drawn there. She was nameless but that her name was woman. Her thighs would seize him in the grips of passion. And he would top her in the hope that she would house his name and pass his bloodline into another generation.

I put the paper down and took my seat again. Stan was silent, but he sat leaning forward. Ursula had her hand on his back and she was staring at me. Pin looked very satisfied. I lifted my glass to my lips, but I didn't drink anything.

"Wow," Stan finally said. "That's powerful stuff. I like it. I really do." He looked back at Ursula.

"It's gruesome," she said. "Tonight, it's gruesome. I feel violated myself." All of us laughed, even Pin.

"You never felt violated before," I said.

"That's because he was always winning women, one way or another."

"It's just another means, another way."

"I like it," Stan repeated and reached for his drink. "I wouldn't mind hearing more some time."

"Well," I said. "My first fan. I might have some

110

more of this section done tomorrow. You're welcome to join us here any night."

"Thanks."

"I won't have you corrupting his mind," Ursula said, half kiddingly, of course.

We were all quiet for a while. The heat of the fire threw a warm glow over everything. I put on some music and we all had another drink and then another. For the first time that night, I was enjoying myself, feeling relaxed and good. When Stan talked now, he talked to me as well as Ursula. I think it bothered her a little because whenever it looked as though the two of us were going to develop a topic, she would try to change the subject. I suddenly found myself thinking, I like him.

I don't remember how many drinks I finally did have. I got so involved in some conversations that I lost count. Whatever the amount, it eventually put me asleep. I awoke suddenly on the couch. Pin was staring at me in silence. I wiped my eyes and sat up. Ursula and Stan were gone. The record on the stereo must have been scratched because the needle was caught in a groove and the same line was playing over and over. It was half past three in the morning.

"What the hell happened?"

"I think you passed out, more or less."

"Jesus," I said, stretching. "What a way to end the evening. That guy must have felt stupid. I just conked out on him, huh?"

"Well, in a way. You began to doze while he and Ursula were dancing. He did pretty well for a guy with a wooden foot, I might add. Don't you remember that?"

"Yes. Vaguely."

"And then you drifted off."

"Yeah. You want to go to your room?"

"No," he said. Sometimes he liked sleeping in that easy chair in the living room. I don't see how it could have been comfortable for that length of time, but he liked it.

"Well, then I guess I'll go up and sleep in a bed."

"Good night."

I walked up the stairs quietly, not wanting to wake Ursula. I didn't even put the light on in my room, because I remembered the adjoining door had been opened earlier and I figured it was probably still open. But when I got into the room and sat on the bed to take off my shoes, I saw that the door had been closed. I figured she had closed it expecting that I would put the light on when I came up. I didn't really need it, though, because the moonlight was so bright, it threw a silvery glow over everything. I got undressed quickly and pulled back the covers. Just before I slipped under them, I heard the sound. It puzzled me for a moment, but then I recognized it to be Ursula's bedsprings. My imagination did flip-flops as I quickly envisioned the possible scene. I debated whether or not I should just ignore it and try to sleep, or whether I should go to that door and open it just enough to look into her room.

I experienced anger, but at the same time, a kind of erotic excitement passed through my body. Finally I could contain myself no longer. With exaggerated slow and careful motions, I slipped out of the bed and inched my way to the door. When I got there, I found it wasn't closed all the way after all. Ursula did that deliberately, I thought. It was her way of inviting me. I could hear her moaning softly. I could hear him grunting. So I opened the door further and peered inside. The moonlight illuminated the upper

and lower portions of his naked back. He seemed to have a radiance all his own. Ursula's moving legs and thighs writhed and rubbed against his body. They moved with well-coordinated rhythmic movements. I got hard watching them. When I could take it no longer, I backed away, and then, after a moment's hesitation, closed the door firmly enough so that she would know I had been there. It worked, because they grew silent immediately. I went back to my bed and slipped under the covers, turning my back on the door.

"That damn Pin," I said aloud, "he didn't tell me. He let me walk up here, while all the while he knew."

It was the first time that I thought he had done something to deliberately hurt me. It was a part of his personality I hadn't experienced, you see. It was surprising. Perhaps, I thought, the whole thing was funny to him. I would have to lead him to believe that when it came to Ursula and her relationships with other men, nothing was to be treated lightly. It was all very serious. As far as I was concerned, very serious.

Chapter 9

I HEARD HIM GET UP VERY EARLY IN THE MORNING AND quietly leave her room. I lay there looking up at the ceiling, listening to him descend the stairs and open and close the front door. He had a distinct clip-clop because of that leg and the resultant limp. After a while the door between my room and Ursula's opened slowly. Out of the corner of my eye, I could see it moving, but I kept looking up. She stepped quietly into my room, holding a small blanket to her naked body.

"Leon? Are you awake?"

"Yeah, I'm awake." I didn't look at her. She moved a little closer to me.

"How do you feel? You had a lot to drink last night."

116

"OK." I looked at her. Her right breast was entirely visible. I turned back on my side and faced the wall. She moved up to my bed and sat at my feet.

"You sort of passed out on us."

"I know. Pin told me."

"I thought you'd end up sleeping down there all night."

"No, you didn't," I said sharply.

"Yes, I did. I would have been sure to close the door completely otherwise." I turned and looked at her. "I mean it."

"Don't bullshit me, Ursula. You never could and you never will."

"What do you mean?" she said straightening up and looking as innocent as she could. What an actress, I thought. I almost broke out laughing in her face.

"You did that deliberately. You just wanted me to hear and see you having inter . . . screwing," I said. I felt a great sense of liberation using the word.

"What's the difference?" she said. "I would have told you all about it anyway." She dropped the blanket and played with her hair, pulling it back behind her head and looking across the room at the mirror above the dresser. Her breasts, pulled upward by the lifting of her arms above her shoulders, became firm and full-looking. I was amazed at her blatantly indifferent attitude. "You haven't seen too many girls built like me, have you, Leon?"

"A few."

"Who?"

"What's the difference?"

"I was just wondering, that's all. You know," she said, turning away and looking back toward her own

bedroom, "once during the night I touched the wooden part of his leg and I got the craziest sensation."

"What do you mean by craziest sensation?"

"It's hard to explain. It was almost like, like touching Pin," she said blushing. "You know, the way . . . the way we used to."

"So? I don't understand why that would be a crazy sensation," I said quickly, in a harsh tone of voice.

"Nothing. It's too hard to explain what I mean, I guess."

"So don't start talking about it then." I felt myself growing more and more irritable by the moment.

"I'm sorry. We all had a great time, though. Stan really likes you."

"I'll bet."

"He does, and he thinks your poem is great."

"Yeah. Why didn't he stay for breakfast? He wasn't afraid to face me after a night in your bed, was he?"

"Don't be ridiculous. He just had to get back, that's all. He's coming around later this afternoon. I was thinking we'd take a ride up to Sam's Point."

"Sam's Point. Only tourists go there. You gotta pay to look off a mountaintop."

"I know. But I just couldn't think of anyplace else to go. It does have a great view, doesn't it?"

"How would I know?"

"You went parking up there once. I think it was with Debbie Wall, don't you remember?"

"I don't remember. I might have."

"You did," she said. She turned around and poked me in the ribs. "You gonna get up or sleep all day?"

"I'll get up, I'll get up. Just whip up some breakfast and you'll see," I said. She leaned over and kissed me on the forehead.

"What's that for?"

"For being so nice to Stan," she whispered. "I knew you would be."

"Sure, sure."

"Hey, maybe you could call someone up and we could make it a double date."

"To Sam's Point? Forget it."

"It was just a thought. I bet it would be fun. Don't you get the Need anymore?"

I turned and looked at her. She had a very serious, almost motherly expression on her face.

"Not any more than usual."

"It's funny," she said, "but I always felt guilty having sex. Not because I thought it was wrong or anything like that, but because I felt bad that you weren't having any at the same time. It's hard to explain."

"That's ridiculous."

"I know, but I feel it nevertheless."

"Go on, go down and make breakfast. Make a couple of sexy poached eggs." She laughed and stood up.

"I really wish you'd seriously consider going along with us."

"It's out of the question. Stop worrying about me. I'll be all right."

"Are you sure?"

"Of course I'm sure. What are you getting at?"

"Nothing. OK. Come on down in about ten minutes."

I watched her walk out of the room and then I turned back to the wall. I lay there thinking no real

thoughts. Finally I got up and took a shower. When I looked out of my bedroom window afterward, I saw that a light snow had begun. It got heavier as we ate breakfast.

"If it keeps up like this, you'd better stay away from Sam's Point. That's a steep incline and there are many windy turns. It's dangerous traveling, even for a man with two good legs."

"Where can we go?"

"Don't go anywhere. Why do you have to go anywhere?"

"I just thought we should take a ride."

"Do what you want. Pin's still asleep?"

"I guess so. Don't you know?"

"I just assumed he was," I said. I called to him. He was awake, so I brought him in for some coffee. He'd only drink a little, but that's all he required in the morning.

I was upstairs when Stan arrived. I heard Ursula let him in. As I started down, I heard the beginning of their conversation. I stopped because it was all about me.

"Ursula, it's far worse than you described. You've got to be kiddin' me and yourself as well. This is no silly little situation. He's as loony as can be."

"Oh, no, really . . ."

"I mean, I don't believe he functions as well as you say he does."

"But he does. He handles all our finances. I'd be lost without him. I even turn my check over to him every two weeks and he does all the banking and investing."

"For Christ sakes . . ." There was a pause and then I heard Stan laugh and say, "Hello, Pin. How

are you, Pin? Feel kind of stiff, do you? Pip, pip, old Pin."

"Shh, stop it, Stan. He's liable to hear you. Please," she said, but she laughed. She sounded like she was being tickled.

I stood there for a moment more, feeling as though someone had slapped me sharply on the face. Ursula conniving against me? It can't be. But then I remembered how matter-of-factly Stan had reacted to Pin and Pin's cold stare. Ursula must have prompted him. This was a conspiracy. It still is, I thought. She brought him here to destroy my relationship with Pin. My hand got numb very quickly. I lifted it from the bannister and slapped it hard against the side of my leg. I welcomed the stinging sensation. Then I took some deliberately heavy steps and they got very quiet in the living room.

"Hi, Leon," Stan said as I entered. "Feeling better?"

"I wasn't feeling sick. You ready for some chess?" I shouted to Pin, deliberately ignoring Ursula.

"Why shouldn't I be ready?"

"We're going to try Sam's Point anyway," Ursula said.

"Go ahead, but don't call me if you end up hanging off a cliff or get stuck in a ditch," I said, and walked to the chess set. I didn't turn back when they both said good-bye. Ursula said good-bye to Pin.

"Yes," Stan said, "good-bye, Pin."

I stood there in the center of the living room with the chessboard in my hands. I heard the front door slam and then I turned to Pin. He could see the outrage in my face immediately. I was a little put out

at him for permitting them to mock me in his presence.

"You look like you're about to have a brain hemorrhage."

"I feel like it. I was standing just outside this room when they were mocking me."

"Oh, that."

"Yes, that. Why didn't you speak up?"

"I was going to say something," he began, "but then I thought Ursula would take it badly, so I just ignored it."

"Thanks."

"What's the big deal? There's no real harm done."

"No real harm done! That was my sister in here. She left with him."

"Take it easy. Maybe you ought to pour yourself a drink."

"I ought to. I ought to be good and stewed when they come back. That bastard, and Ursula, that bitch."

"You gonna play chess or mumble to yourself all the rest of the day?"

I did pour myself a drink and we did play chess. It was a long game. It grew dark outside and we were still at it. I forgot all about supper, having no real appetite anyway. Along about seven-thirty, I realized that Ursula and Stan had probably gone out to eat, so I went into the kitchen and fixed myself a turkey sandwich. Pin just wanted to nibble on a little of the roast beef from the night before. I watched some television, but after a while Pin got real sleepy, so I had to wheel him into his bedroom. Then I turned off the set and went upstairs to read in bed. I

fell asleep and awoke a little after one in the morning. I heard the car door slam outside and peered out the window. It was a dark night with some overcast, but I could make out Ursula and Stan coming toward the house. I got up and listened at the top of the stairs.

"Leon's probably gone to sleep," she said.

"I wonder if Pin did too," he said, and there was that giggling again. God, it made me mad.

"How about a nightcap?" she said, and he agreed. They went into the living room. I walked down the stairs until I could hear their voices clearly. They were still talking about me. Ursula sounded like a different person when she was alone with him.

"How long have you had this 'friend,' Pin, living here?" he asked.

"As long as we've been alone. We brought him here the same day my uncles and aunts left us."

"And was Leon always so attached to him? I mean, it? Even before your parents' death?"

"Oh, yes. He used to go over to the office by himself and talk to him. Especially at night, when he could be alone there."

"Well, I hate to harp on it, but something's got to be done. And soon, Ursula. He's still a young guy. I'm sure they could help him."

"They?"

"Psychiatrists. He needs to be institutionalized. It's a real shame because he does seem intelligent and creative. I like his poetry."

"You're perverted, just like he is," she said.

I couldn't believe she said it. Then I wondered about all the things she probably had said when they were alone in his car. It was a shock to hear Ursula

talk against me. I realized that she might have done that many times before. At first, I felt real hurt and sad, but as I listened to them, I got angry.

"You don't get frightened living here like this? I mean, who knows what's going on in his mind."

"Frightened? Oh, no." She laughed. "What's there to be afraid of? Leon wouldn't hurt me and I'm sure Pin wouldn't." She laughed again, and then he laughed.

So, she's not afraid of Pin, I thought. What's more, she even thinks it's silly to contemplate being afraid of him, huh? All right, I thought, we'll see about that. Pin has got quite a temper when he gets going. He's not going to like the way things are turning out, not when I tell him what else I heard. Oh no, he's going to be just as indignant and as outraged as I am, I thought.

"I'm probably not the first person you've brought home to meet Pin," Stan said, in a very low, seductive voice. There was a long pause. Probably kissing, I thought.

"That's where you're wrong," she said. I could hardly hear her now. "It's been a long time since I brought anyone home with me."

I took a few steps down and got closer to the doorway. I peered through the crack between the door and the wall. They were sitting on the couch, sitting very close together. He had a drink in his hand, but he leaned over and put it down on the table.

"I'll tell you one thing," he said. "I'm glad you warned me about all this. Otherwise, I would have slipped away the first chance I got."

"That's why I warned you," she said, and they kissed a long kiss. She leaned back against the arm

of the couch. He sprawled over her and I watched them squirm around on the couch for a while. Then I turned and walked back upstairs, very quietly. My worst fears were realized. Ursula had connived against me. I just couldn't believe it.

There had been so few times in our lives when we were truly at odds with each other. I know that was unusual for a brother and sister growing up with only a couple of years separating them, but I always believed we had a deep understanding of each other's wants and needs and this was primarily responsible for our good relationship. Occasionally we fought over a toy or some dumb privilege like sitting in the front seat of the car, but both of us were always so sensitive to the other's feelings. I couldn't take her being unhappy for too long and she never seemed to be able to take my being unhappy. We were so tuned in to each other's moods. What had happened now to destroy that closeness, that awareness?

I searched my mind for the memory of anything that could justify her doing what she was doing. There was nothing, no reason for her to suddenly turn against me, be intimate with a complete stranger and confide in him at my expense. There was no reason except her own insatiable lust. The Need, I thought. It's turned her against me. Her Need is so great that she'd do anything to have that man in her bed, even ridicule me, make up lies about me and Pin. Damn her, I thought, damn her and her damn Need.

Then I thought, poor Pin, lying there in his bed, unaware that Ursula had turned against us. She was mocking us with a stranger. It's going to kill him when he finds out all the rest. He always had the

deepest regard for Ursula, many times taking her side against me, in fact. He won't believe she's betrayed him, betrayed us. It's going to upset him for quite a while; he's going to just sulk. But then, he's going to get angry. I've seen it happen before. He's going to want to punish her in some way.

Pin and I will have to discuss it, I thought. We'll have to have an intelligent discussion. Firstly, I'm going to have to figure a way to end this romance. I was glad that I hadn't made a mistake about her soldier boy. Pin's going to be upset about that too. He doesn't like being wrong about people.

So he would have slipped away the first chance he got, huh? I said to myself. Well, he's going to wish he had. Yessir, I said, slapping my fist into the palm of my hand, he's going to wish that he had. I crawled under the covers, muttering threats, and I was still lying there awake, my eyes open, staring up into the darkness, when Ursula came quietly up the stairs and went to bed.

Chapter 10

THE NEXT MORNING I SAID NOTHING TO URSULA ABOUT what I had overheard. My decision was not to confront her directly with it. That, I thought, might only make her more secretive in the future. She was her usual pleasant self at breakfast, maybe a little more so. I figured that she was trying to show me how much happier she had become since meeting and going out with Stan. She hummed and flitted around the kitchen with this big smile on her face. It was hard for me to keep composed and put aside my angry feelings. Pin wasn't awake yet. He would have sensed something wrong with me right away. He was always good at that, especially when it came to me.

"I suppose," I said, "Stan will be coming to the library today."

"Only at the end of the day. He's taking me to see his mother. He wants me to meet her."

"What happened to his great study of Far Eastern religion?"

"Nothing," she said, but she didn't elaborate.

"Are you sure he wasn't just using that as an excuse to get to know you?"

"What if he was?" She didn't look at me.

"So. And now he wants you to meet his mother before she kicks off."

"Don't be so crude, Leon. No, not before she dies. That's not why. He just wants me to meet her and her to meet me."

"Sounds serious."

"It could become serious," she said, pausing and thinking for a moment. "When I'm with him, I feel very relaxed, very good."

"Do you? That's interesting. I would imagine he would be the type to make you nervous. I mean, considering all that he's been through and all that's happened to him."

"No, he's not that way. He's . . . well, he's just a very sincere individual," she said. I was quiet for the rest of the time. I was burning up inside, containing all the anger. After she left, I broke the dish she had eaten off. I smashed it into pieces by slamming it hard into the sink. That noise woke Pin. I heard him call for me.

I helped him dress and wheeled him out to the kitchen. I could see from the way he was staring at me that he realized something was very wrong, but he waited for a while. I served him his coffee and

poured myself another cup. Then we made some small talk for a while. He complained about his legs again. I complained about my hand. The joints of his knees always ached in the morning.

"I had the heating pads on all night," he said. "I had a hard time falling asleep."

"Then maybe you heard some of what went on in the living room last night, huh?"

"Went on? What went on?"

"Ursula and her soldier boy returned a little after one o'clock. They sat on the couch talking. I overheard them."

"Not again."

"Yes, again. This time I heard Ursula."

"What do you mean?"

"She connived against us. She told him about you, prepared him in a way. Gave him information how he should react and behave in our presence."

"She didn't."

"I heard him say so. They talked about us both as if we were lunatics. She told him some very private things about us. I know, I know, it's hard to believe, but she did."

"She must really like him."

"That doesn't justify it."

"I didn't say it did. Wow. I thought he was a bit too cool."

"Oh, he's cool all right. He probably figures on eventually taking things over around here. He's got her convinced that we're sick, mentally sick. I know just what he's planning to do."

"What?"

"Marry Ursula and get us committed some-where."

"She wouldn't go for that. She wouldn't . . ."

"She ridicules you. She talks about you as if you . . . as if you didn't really exist, had no mind. I don't know what to think about her. I've been wondering, though, Pin. Could she have felt this way for a long time? Has she been humoring us with her attention and concern? Tell the truth, did Ursula ever talk to you like I do?"

"Sure, what do you mean?"

"I mean, lately, has she acted the same way she used to act with you?"

"Well, you're always around. Well, I . . ."

"That's what I thought. She tells me she talks to you, comes down to see you, spends time with you in your room, but she's just been saying that to humor me and keep me believing she still cares about us. She's been lying."

"I can't believe it. You actually heard her say these things?"

"With my own ears. How do you think I felt?"

"I'd never think of Ursula being false to us."

"I know how you feel. How did we lose her, Pin?"

"I don't know. When I think of some of those long conversations we used to have when she was younger . . . it makes me mad. It really does."

"I've been trying not to hate her, but it's hard."

"It's hard," he said. We were both quiet for a while. I drank my coffee and sat there thinking. I could tell that he was very upset. He glared ahead. Not a muscle moved in his face.

"So?" I said finally. "What do we do now?"

"We must punish her, punish her for being unfaithful, and we must restore her faith in us."

"Yes. I agree."

"This man is taking up all her time and energy now. He's commanding her full attention. Whatever he says about us, she's going to accept."

"That's just what I thought."

"We've got to get her to challenge him and see what he truly is."

"I knew you'd know what to do, Pin. I knew it."

"She's got to feel my full presence again, become dependent upon me and believe in me the way she used to."

"Right. So where do we start?" I asked. His determination was giving me new confidence.

"We begin immediately. We begin right here at home," he added, and I pulled my chair closer to him and listened as he began to unravel his plan to win back Ursula.

He was full of ideas. What he suggested called for some equipment and materials. I had to go out and make some purchases, but every one of his plans was good. He was a very creative person and very inventive. I don't know how Ursula could have lost faith in him to the extent that she would betray him. There was no one like him, no one as intelligent, as charming, or as interesting. She was a fool. His idea now was to shock her and punish her. She deserved it. I couldn't wait to get started.

Stan dropped her off about nine-thirty that night. I was in the living room with Pin watching television. We looked at each other when she opened the front door and entered. "Now it begins," I whispered. He nodded.

"Hi," she said from the doorway. I turned to her.

"Hi. Come on in and tell us about your visit."

"Oh, it was very bad. She's terribly sick. She could die any day, any minute, actually."

"Is that so?" Pin said. I could see in his face and hear in his tone of voice that he was having the same difficulty I was having in controlling his anger.

"Is that why he brought you home so early?"

"Yes. I don't feel so well either. I think I'll just go up and soak in a hot tub for a while."

"Good idea," I said. I turned back to the television. She went upstairs. A moment later I heard her call down to me. "What is it?" I yelled. I had been waiting. Pin smiled.

"What's this box on the wall outside of your bedroom and mine?"

"It's an intercom."

"Intercom? What for?"

"It's for Pin," I said, walking to the foot of the stairs. "It'll make it easier for him to call if he needs us."

"Oh. How come you never thought of it before?"

"He never needed us as much before," I said, but she didn't get my subtle meaning.

"Very clever," she sang out and went to her bath. When I walked back to the living room, Pin was still smiling. She didn't know how clever he really was. There was the one intercom she saw on the wall and there was the one in Pin's room, right by his bed. But there was also one in my room, right under my bed.

"Let's do the recording now," I said. "She's taking a bath."

"Fine. You sure that little machine will have enough volume?"

"Positive. I tried it out in the store first," I said, taking the pocket tape recorder out of my pants pocket. It was just a little bigger than the palm of my hand. "We won't need that much volume anyway.

The intercoms have a volume control too and I've got the one outside of her room turned way up."

"Good. Let's get on with it."

He recorded the message in his voice, a voice remarkably like my father's. It was a simple message. He continually called for Ursula to come down to him. I recorded about six or seven minutes of it. I didn't think we needed much more. If she didn't hear it the first time, I would simply rewind and play it over and over until she did. When we were finished, I put the machine back into my pocket.

"I'll wait until she's just about to fall asleep and then I'll begin. I'd let you do it right through the intercom, but like you said, you wouldn't know when to begin, and it will look a lot better for us if I'm upstairs when it happens."

"No question about it. We've got to do this right. That man's planted doubts, and he will continue to do so. She'll get to the point where she's completely dependent upon him and free of us. We've got to do this, even though it's unpleasant for all of us."

"And what if she does come down to you?"

"I'll be waiting on the couch. You've got the luminous paint?"

"Right."

"OK. On my fingers and around my eyes."

"Sure it won't do you any harm?"

"Positive," he said, so I painted it on just the way he wanted me to. Before I went up, I put out the lights and looked at him. It was terrific, just like he said it would be. His fingers seemed like they were resting in midair and his eyes were deep holes of darkness, accented by the luminous circles around them. I laughed.

"This is just the beginning," he said. "We've got a lot more to do."

"I know. See you later."

"See you later," he said. I walked upstairs slowly, encouraged by my vision of Ursula's panic. She would come running to me in her desperate need to be comforted. She was still in the bathtub. I tried the door, but it was locked. She hadn't done that before. I knocked.

"You all right in there?"

"Yes. I'm just about finished drying off," she added. "I'll be right out."

"Need any help? Want me to dry your back?"

"No, it's all right. Thanks."

"Suit yourself," I said and went to my room. I sat at my desk and tried rewriting some lines of the poem that didn't please me, but I couldn't concentrate. I kept touching the pocket tape recorder and thinking about the plan. Pin was waiting patiently downstairs. That's one thing about him, I thought; he has great patience. He never loses his cool. I sat back and took a deep breath. "Try to be like Pin," I told myself. "Try to be like Pin."

Out of the corner of my eye, I saw myself in the mirror. I was sitting stiffly in the chair, my back pressed hard against the back of it, my shoulders pulled up and my head held stiffly erect. I would have sat that way for quite a while, but I heard Ursula come into her room. "Got to act completely natural," I told myself. "Don't let her get a bit suspicious." So I got up and opened the door. She was sitting on her bed with a towel around her hair. Other than that, she was completely naked. Her skin was pinkish from the hot water.

135

"How do you feel now?"

"A lot better. It really was terrible, Leon. It made me feel creepy all over."

"I know what you mean. I once came into the office right after an old man died. The doctor didn't have him covered or anything."

"Ugh. I'm glad I wasn't with you."

"He was just sitting there talking to Pin about the case. He was very calm and matter-of-fact about it. The man had a heart attack in the office, actually out in the lobby. They were waiting for someone to come and get the body. I remember how the man's hand was just hanging stiffly off the table. His fingers were cupped like he expected someone to come over and put something in them."

"The doctor was so crude sometimes, wasn't he?"

"He was just scientific, unattached, uninvolved."

"I think that's crude."

"I'm sure your boyfriend saw a lot of dead people and got to the point where he just looked at them matter-of-factly."

"Never. Stan's too sensitive to be matter-of-fact about death."

"Maybe. You want to talk about him?"

"No," she said. I thought she said it rather quickly and emphatically.

"Why not?"

"I'm just not in the mood. Visiting his mother and all," she added, more to placate me than anything else.

"Suit yourself." I turned to leave, but she called me back.

"Leon, Stan asked me how come you don't have any girl friends over. He thought that if you did,

maybe we could do some double dates. It might be
fun."

"My love life is none of his damn business."

"He didn't ask to be nosy. He only thought . . ."

"I know what he thought," I said, forgetting my
self-control. "He thought it unnatural for me to stay
here and not have the outside interests you have,
isn't that it?"

"He never said you were unnatural. Really, Leon,
we were just thinking of ways to have some fun."

"I'll bet."

"What's wrong? You look so tense, so twisted up
and ugly inside."

"Nothing. I just don't like people talking about
me, that's all. When I want someone, I'll go out and
get her. I never lacked the ability to do so, did I?"

"Never. You were always a big lover." She
smiled.

"So? Why concern yourself then?"

"Come over here and sit next to me. Why won't
you come?" she added when I hesitated.

"What do you want?"

"Just come over. How about giving me a mas-
sage? My kidneys ache again," she said and turned
to sprawl out on her stomach. I looked at her for a
moment. I knew what she was trying to do—she was
trying to soften me up. I walked over and sat on the
bed. "Come on," she said. I began rubbing her back
in small circles and then larger ones. "Oh, that's
good."

"Can't you get Stan to do this?"

"He's not here now. Anyway, you know just how
to do it and you have such strong hands."

"Thanks."

"You do," she said, propping herself up on her right elbow.

"OK, OK, I do." She sprawled out again. I watched her ass move under the rhythm of my hands. It had such a nice shape to it and such fullness. I moved over and over it and then down to her thighs, inside them and around the legs. She moaned and groaned, lying there with her eyes closed, her lips pursed. It did have a relaxing effect on me too. I felt less tense and annoyed for the moment.

"Remember when you came in here and did this to Miriam Cohen?"

"Yeah, I remember. It seems like a hundred years ago already."

"It does."

"A lot of things have changed since then," I said, playing around with double meanings again. She didn't say anything. I worked down her legs to the calves and then stopped by slapping her on the ass.

"Ouch," she said, turning over on her back. I got up and started for my bedroom again. "Where are you going?"

"To sleep. I'm tired."

"Will you think about it at least?"

"About what?"

"Stan's suggestion."

"Yeah, I'll think about it. Sure, why not?"

"Sherry Chester is always asking about you. Whenever I see her, she asks how you are and what you're doing."

"That slut."

"She's a nice girl now. Works as a secretary for Jack Bernstein."

"Probably putting out for him. She put out for everybody in high school."

"Think about it, will you, Leon?"

"I said I would, didn't I? Listen, what the hell is this supposed to be anyway, Rehabilitate Leon Week?" I said, and I slammed the door closed between us. I stood there smiling on my side. I had been worrying about how I was going to close that door.

Chapter 11

I WAITED ONE HOUR AFTER I HEARD URSULA GET INTO BED
to go to sleep. Then I took the tape recorder, just as
we had planned, and I turned on my intercom. Over
and over Pin's voice began to play through the
speakers. I watched the door between Ursula's room
and mine. I waited for her light to go on. I felt some
pangs of regret doing it. I readily admit that, but
taunting her with Pin's voice was part of both her
punishment and her treatment. We had to win her
back completely. There was no other way. I just
used father's old standby expression—"The pain is
the price we pay for recovery." His voice went on.

"Ursula, Ursula, come down, I need you. I want
to talk to you. Ursula, Ursula, come down. Please,

142

Ursula, come down. Ursula, Ursula, come down, I need you. Please."

It ran through twice and still there was no reaction from her. It worried me, but I kept it up. I can't fail now, I thought. Pin's waiting downstairs. He's been waiting all night. Again, we'll play it again and again. I began to sweat a little in anticipation. Finally, I grew impatient with the machine. It was as if no voice were coming over it. Maybe something went wrong when I played the tape recorder into the intercom, I thought. Then, in the best disguised voice I could manage, I spoke through the intercom, saying the exact things Pin had recorded. I did that for only a little while when the light went on in Ursula's room.

I waited, lying back in my bed, closing my eyes, and pretending to be fast asleep. The door opened slowly. I opened my eyes slightly. She stood there peering in at me. She was dressed in her nightgown and holding her hands to her chest. She stood waiting for the longest time. I think she wanted to be sure I was asleep. Then she closed the door and went back to bed, satisfied, probably, that she had dreamt the whole thing. I smiled to myself and reached for the intercom again.

"Ursula, Ursula, come down, I need you. I want to talk to you. Ursula, Ursula, come down. Please, Ursula, come down. Ursula, Ursula, come down, I need you. Please."

Her light went on again. I shut off the intercom and took the same position. She opened the door abruptly, as if she had hoped to catch me at something. But there I was, lying back in bed, my eyes closed, my breathing regular. She stood there

so long this time that I had to act as if she woke me up. I turned with feigned surprise.

"What? What is it? What's the matter? What the hell's the matter?" She continued to just stand there looking in at me. "Jesus, you scared the shit out of me, Ursula. What's the matter, damnit?"

"Didn't you hear anything?"

"What?"

"A . . . a voice, someone's voice?"

"I was in a deep sleep. Shit, I was having a nice dream and I was in a deep sleep. What's this all about?"

"I'm frightened, Leon. I heard a voice."

"Aw, come on, will you . . . a voice . . . wait, a voice?"

"Yes, did you hear it then?"

"No, but maybe it was Pin," I said. "It's probably only Pin." I said it very matter-of-factly. She stood there looking at me. "Don't you suppose so?"

"I—I don't know."

"What did the voice say? Did you hear any words?"

"Yes. It kept calling my name."

"So? It's probably Pin and he probably wants to see you, that's all," I said lying back again. "Just go downstairs and see what he wants."

"Leon," she called sharply, "it wasn't Pin." I sat up and looked at her.

"What?"

"It wasn't Pin. It couldn't have been Pin."

"Why not? Who else could it have been?"

"I don't know."

"Look, Ursula, just go downstairs and see what he wants."

"I'm not going. You go, if you're so sure it was

Pin," she said, and she turned around and went back to bed, but this time she left the door opened between our two rooms. That was bad because if I turned the intercom on and spoke, she'd hear it coming from my room as well as from right outside her bedroom door. I'd have to either get up and close the door, or else forget about it for the night.

I got up, pretending to be concerned. Then I put the light on in my room and walked into her bedroom. She looked at me from under her covers. I stood listening impatiently.

"I don't hear a thing. How come I don't hear the voice too?"

"It stopped when I got up. Just wait awhile and listen."

"OK," I said, and I sat by the foot of her bed and waited for ten full minutes. Both of us were completely silent. There were some creaks in the building and the sounds made by the wind outside. Then I got up and walked to the window. The night sky was overcast. It was pitch black out there.

"You see anyone out there?"

"Can't. It's so damn dark I can't even see the road."

"All right," she said. "Forget about it. It's probably only my imagination."

"Just a dream, you think?" I walked over to her and touched her face. She held my hand to her. Poor Ursula, I thought, poor little Ursula. It's too bad, but we have to do these things to you. I remembered her when she was small and sweet, fully dependent upon me. We were so good to each other then. Things were right; things were as they should be. "Don't worry, I'm here," I said. She kissed my hand and then she turned over and closed her eyes.

I stood looking down at her for a few more moments and then I walked out, taking care to close the door between us. I waited, afraid that she would call out and ask me to open it again. But she didn't. I smiled to myself and put out my lights. Then I went back to bed and I lay there for a good half an hour, waiting. It was important to be patient, to do the right thing at the right time. Pin had made that perfectly clear when we planned the whole thing out. I wanted her to fall asleep again, to be awakened from a deep sleep. She'd lie there in the dark, listening, waiting to be sure that what she heard was real and not imagined. Then fear would grow.

I was ready again. I leaned over and turned on the intercom. In a voice that made me think of my father, I repeated the words. I did it slowly and clearly, keeping an eye on the door for the first sign of a light in her room.

"Ursula, Ursula, come down, I need you. I want to talk to you. Ursula, Ursula, come down. Please, Ursula, come down. Ursula, Ursula, come down, I need you. Please."

She didn't get up and put on her lights. I suppose she was probably too frightened to move. She just lay there in the dark listening and wondering. The darkness oppressed her. She was probably sweating. I could imagine her all crouched up, in the fetal position, pressed against the wall. I kept calling through the intercom. I don't know how long I called, but finally, tired myself, I turned it off and went to sleep. She was still sleeping in the morning when I got up, so I went downstairs quietly and helped Pin get settled in his seat in the living room. I had to wash off the luminous paint. We didn't get to

see it used, but we felt the first stage of our plan had still been effective. I then went upstairs to wake her for work. She was oversleeping because she was probably up most of the night.

"Hey," I said, standing in the doorway, "you getting up today, or should I call Miss Spartacus and tell her you're not feeling well?"

"No, I'll be getting up," she said wiping her eyes. She just continued to lie there, thinking.

"You sure?"

"Yes."

"Oh," I said casually, as I turned to go back downstairs, "that voice you heard last night?"

"Yes." She looked at me with great anticipation.

"It was Pin all right. He just told me. He wanted to talk to you and he was hoping you were still awake." She didn't say anything. She continued to stare out at me. "I told you it was probably Pin, didn't I?"

"And what did he want to talk to me about?" she asked after a few moments of silence.

"How should I know? You know the way Pin is. If he had something to say to you, he wanted to say it to you. You'll have to ask him yourself."

"Well, why did he keep calling me? Once I didn't answer, why didn't he stop?" she said quickly, as if she had found a hole in my story.

"He thought you were probably in my room or in the bathroom. He still doesn't believe in that intercom anyway," I said. "He can't imagine his voice traveling through it well. You'll have to tell him how well it works."

"Yes, I'll have to," she said. She turned and looked up at the ceiling. Then I left her.

That night she brought Stan home with her. She had obviously described to him what had occurred the night before. He very quietly and unobtrusively inspected the intercom outside of her bedroom door. Then he asked me where the other one was located.

"I don't see it in the living room here," he said.

"No, it's in Pin's room."

"Can I see it?"

"Pin doesn't like anyone going into his room. He doesn't even let the cleaning woman in there."

"Oh? That's a wireless set you've got there, isn't it?"

"Yes. I didn't want to have wires running all over the place."

"I don't blame you." Ursula called to say that supper was ready, so I went into Pin's room to get him.

"She told him all about last night," I said.

"Didn't you expect that she would?"

"He was snooping around."

"No question, he's going to be trouble. We've got to work fast."

"Yeah, well, don't be surprised if she has him stay overnight tonight."

"If so, we'll have to wait. Don't take any chances with him around."

"Right," I said, and we went to dinner. Everyone was pleasant to everyone else, but I knew what they were hiding behind those phony smiles. Pin was cordial, but not really friendly. Only I could notice the innuendo, the intimation, the subtle strain in his voice and glances. Ursula was too busy doting on Stan to notice anything else. After dinner Stan asked me if I had any more of the poem done. I couldn't

see the harm in letting him hear the new verse, so I went up and got it. We all sat around the fire again, only this time Pin sat further into the shadows.

"As you might remember," I began, "Testes was about to rape a woman."

"Oh, yes, I remember," Stan said shooting a glance at Ursula. I could see she was suppressing a giggle, but I ignored it.

"Well," I said, "something stops him for a moment, makes him hesitate."

"What?"

"You'll see." I began.

Closer, closer, closer she came to him, moving, it seemed, in silent motion. He thought to kiss the lips between her thighs. His heart beat steadily within the caverns of his bosom, driving hot blood thick down, down into the depths of his loins. He thought he caught the odor of a familiar perfume. And then, like the predator he had become, he lunged from the deepest darkest passions in us all. She turned without a sound and faced him. He stopped abruptly. It was as if a knife had performed instant castration. He was looking into the eyes of his sister.

I set the manuscript down and took my seat. Both of them were quiet. Pin, of course, had heard the verses before. We both waited for their reactions, but they were slow in coming. Ursula stared at me with a look of confusion on her face. Stan acted as if he were seeing me for the first time. I cleared my throat and lifted my glass to my lips.

"Well," Stan began, looking at Ursula first and then turning back to me, "that's a surprise twist, all right."

"Yes," I said, "it is. Now I have to decide whether he retreats back into the darkness or continues on his course."

"And rapes her? His own sister?" Stan said.

"Why not?" I looked at Ursula when I said it. She looked away. "Of course, he probably would kill her as well."

"This thing's getting a bit too deep for me," he said, smiling.

"Yes," I said, "it can get deep, very deep. You don't have a brother or sister, do you, Stan?"

"I had a younger brother, but he died from a blood disease. He only lived to eleven."

"I didn't know. Ursula never told me."

"I don't talk about him much. It was sad."

"I understand," I said. "Were you close?"

"As close as two brothers could be."

"He doesn't want to talk about it, Leon," Ursula said.

"I'm sorry." There was a long silence, so I got up and put on some music. "Why don't you two dance?" I said, pretending to have forgotten all about Stan's leg.

"Good idea," Ursula said quickly. He could do the slow things all right, but the fast ones made him look pathetic. I sat there smiling, occasionally looking over to Pin and nodding. He was very patient and very satisfied with the way things were going. We all had another drink. Then Pin said he was tired, so I took him to his room. I figured he just wanted to talk to me alone.

"Good night," Pin said, but neither of them

replied. "Quickly," Pin said as soon as we closed the door, "I want to hear what they say." I opened the door slightly and we listened. Their voices were low, but clear.

"I don't like it," he said. "That poem suggests a violent mind. I don't believe you're safe here with him like this."

"I don't know. I just don't know. I mean, you're right about him, but . . ."

"You can't even get him to come out with you on a date. You said so yourself. You've got to face up to it before it's too late for him."

"I will," she said. "I'll give it more serious thought. I promise. But let's not talk about it anymore. You want to go upstairs? Now's as good a time as any to make our little exit."

"Sure," he said. We heard them get up and leave.

"No question," Pin said. "He's a dangerous influence on her now."

"I hate him. I wish we could speed things up a little."

"No. We've got to move carefully. Looks to me like he's going to be here for quite a while tonight, but maybe he'll have to leave because of his mother."

"Yeah."

"Just be patient, Leon."

Pin was right. It was uncanny the way he could predict the outcome of things sometimes. I used to believe he possessed some sort of supernatural power. I never told Ursula, but a few days before our parents were killed, Pin had this feeling something tragic was about to happen.

Anyway, about an hour after Ursula and Stan went upstairs, the phone rang. I picked it up in the

living room, but Ursula had picked it up in her room too. It was for Stan. His aunt was calling to tell him that she had just called the doctor for his mother. She was in a bad way, having great difficulty breathing. I heard the whole conversation and hung up after he did. Then I went in and told Pin. A great look of satisfaction came over his face.

"Oh, this is perfect," he said. "This is good. This will leave Ursula in one of her frightened states. You know how she gets when anything serious like this happens."

"I'd better get up to her."

"No, just wait. Wait in the living room. Let her call to you. Let her need you."

"Yes," I said. We heard Stan rush out the front door and pull away in his car. Then I walked back into the living room and sat on the couch, waiting. Moments later, Ursula called down to me. I walked to the foot of the stairs and saw her standing naked at the top.

"Come up, Leon. Please, come up."

"Why?"

"I want to talk to you. Stan's mother took a bad turn."

"Oh, I'm sorry. Just let me put out the lights," I said. I watched her turn and go back toward her room. I waited at the stairs for a moment, and then walked up, leaving the lights on deliberately. It was part of the plan. She was sitting in a lotus position on her bed. It was dark, but the glow of the hall light made her skin shine. I walked over to her slowly and sat on the bed.

"When he left, he said this was it."

"That's too bad." I took her hand and we sat there in the dark for a full five minutes without speaking. I

could feel the throb of her heartbeat growing faster as she pressed her wrist against me.

"His mother's going to die," she finally said.

"I understand that."

"I can hear the sound of the dirt hitting mother's coffin."

"Don't start thinking about that now. You know what it does to you."

"Sometimes I wake up at night hearing it. I remember your face. You were standing so still. You looked . . . you looked like Pin."

"I don't want to talk about it."

"The nights . . . the nights were always so quiet afterward, weren't they, Leon?"

"Not any quieter than they were before."

"They were. You know they were, just knowing we were alone in this house. You used to come and stay with me all the time."

"You want me to stay with you tonight?"

"Yes, just for a while, until I fall asleep. Will you?"

"Sure," I said. I got up and put out the hall lights. Then I came into the room and closed the door behind me. There was a little light coming in from the moon reflecting off the snow and ice outside. She was on her back looking up at the ceiling. I sat beside her and I gently stroked her hair. Some time passed. We didn't say a word to one another. I heard him first. That was only natural because I was waiting for him to call. We had planned it that way. I turned quickly.

"What's the matter, Leon?"

"Pin's calling, don't you hear?"

"No, I didn't hear him. What does he want?"

"He wants me to come down."

153

"No, he doesn't, Leon," she said gently. She turned toward me and touched my face, pressing her breasts against me. "Stay with me."

"I'll be just a minute. I've got to see what's the matter." I got off the bed and walked to the door.

"Are you sure he's calling? I don't hear him now," she said. She was really pleading for me to stay. She slipped off the bed too and took a few steps toward me. I opened the door.

"Something's up, all right."

"Why?"

"The lights are on downstairs. Pin had to come out for some reason, and you know how difficult that is for him."

"What?" She came to the door. The light from the living room threw liquid shadows up the ceiling by the stairs. "Maybe you just forgot to put them out," she said. I could hear the note of hysteria building in her voice.

"Don't you remember?" I said, turning. "I put them out right after you called to me. Don't you remember me going back to do it?"

"You're scaring me, Leon."

"There's nothing to be frightened of, Ursula. I'll just go down and see what Pin wants," I said and pulled away from her. She called to me again, but I moved quickly down the stairs and to Pin's room. He was waiting at the door, right where I had left him.

"Everything's all set," I said.

"Good," he said, and I lifted him out of the chair.

Chapter 12

DESPITE HIS HEIGHT AND APPEARANCE IN FATHER'S SUITS, Pin was always very light and easy to carry. I never had any trouble lifting him. We went right to the stairs. I knew Ursula would be waiting right at the top, right where I left her. Although Pin was light, I moved up slowly with ponderous steps. She stepped back, her hand at her mouth, the moment she saw us begin to climb.

"There she is," I whispered.

"Good," he said. "Good."

"What is it, Leon?" she called in a very hoarse, shrill voice. "Why are you bringing Pin upstairs?"

"He wants to be with you tonight," I said. "He knows how you're feeling. He wants to be with you." I drew closer.

156

"But remember? We said we'd never bring him upstairs, Leon. Leon, remember?"

"He wants to be with you, Ursula. We can't deny him. Not after all these years. Just this one night," I said, coming to the top of the stairs. She had backed all the way to her room.

"No," she said. "No, please take him back downstairs, Leon. I don't want him here tonight. Not tonight."

"You're not being very hospitable, Ursula, and not very polite. It's not like you. She's not herself tonight, Pin."

"I know," he said. "That's why I wanted to come up."

"You see, he just wants to help you."

"No," she said again. We had come to her doorway and she had backed up, almost to her bed.

"I don't understand you, Ursula. When mother and the doctor died, who did we go to? Who did we go to see and be with? Who comforted us? It was Pin. Have you forgotten all that?"

"Please, Leon, not tonight. I want to be alone, just with you."

"Pin's quite hurt by all this. That's why he's being so quiet and so patient, I might add. Now, lie down there, Ursula."

"No."

"Lie down. Down."

"Please, Leon, don't do this. Please," she begged. She had backed up against the bed. When I took another step toward her, she sat on it. Her hands were up, cupping her face. "Please," she said again, in a muffled voice. "Please."

As I brought Pin closer, she had to move back on

the bed. She backed all the way to the other side, her back to the wall. I set him down on the bed.

"Now we're all together and safe," I said. I could hear Ursula subdue a sob. "You should really be nicer to Pin, shouldn't you, Ursula? Shouldn't you?" I demanded.

"Yes," she said. Her voice was barely audible.

"What?"

"Yes," she repeated, growing louder.

"Remember how we all used to lie together in bed, with Pin between us?"

"No, no. We decided he wasn't to come upstairs anymore. We decided."

"It was wrong. It was wrong to decide that. I realize it now."

"I'm not going to do it. It was just a game then, something we did to keep ourselves amused, to keep from being lonely."

"It was wrong to make such a decision," I repeated, and I glared at her. "Touch him."

"No."

"TOUCH HIM!" I shouted. She hesitated. I stepped closer to the bed and unbuttoned Pin's jacket. "Touch him," I said in a more pleasant voice. She hesitated, staring up at me. I nodded. "Go ahead, Ursula."

"Please, Leon, please." I stood by waiting. Finally she leaned forward and touched Pin's face as she used to.

"Good. Now help him get undressed."

"Oh, God, no. I don't want to."

"Why not? Because of Stan? Is that why?"

"No, Leon. We stopped doing this so long ago, didn't we? Why start again?" She was trying to sound sweet and understanding.

"Pin thinks we need it."

"He's wrong."

"Has he ever been wrong before when it came to us? Ever?"

"He's wrong this time. Believe me. Take him back down and you come up to stay with me. We'll talk and the night will pass. I promise I'll be all right."

"Help him undress," I repeated, much more firmly. Pin waited passively. Ursula leaned over and took off his jacket. I stood by watching. "That's good, Ursula," I said. "It'll be good, just the way it was." She didn't respond, but she worked a little faster. "Remember you used to say his body was cool, cool against yours? It was good, Ursula, good. It'll be good again." She looked up at me, her eyes wide. I could see the old excitement awakening within her as I resurrected memories. She untied his shoes and took them off. Then she removed the socks. She unbuckled his pants and slid them down, moving slowly and silently. "He's still cool, isn't he? Isn't he?"

"Yes," she said. She didn't look up. "Yes."

I undressed quickly and the three of us lay there naked on the bed. At first there was only the sound of heavy breathing—mine, Pin's and Ursula's. I looked over. Ursula was holding Pin's hand. I thought that was good. Things were going fine. This was the way it was night after night until Ursula rebelled and demanded Pin be kept downstairs again. Sometimes we just fell asleep like this. Most of the time Pin and I had to comfort Ursula. She needed so much attention, so much patience and understanding.

"You want to feel his body against yours," I said. "You want to do that." There was no answer for a

while. I could see her fingers moving nervously in Pin's hand.

"Yes," she whispered.

"It will be like it was."

I helped Pin turn to her slowly. She kept her eyes closed. Carefully I guided him onto her. Then her arms came up gradually, almost as if she had to struggle against some invisible strings holding them down on the bed. She embraced him and she ran her hands up and down his spine. Pin was silent, gentle. I waited.

"Oh, Pin," she said. "I *am* afraid and I *am* lonely."

"There, there," I said. "Pin's here. He's with you."

"Stay with me, Pin."

"Easy. Relax. Easy." Her breathing had quickened. Her head was moving slowly from side to side, her eyes still closed. Her lips were wet. She took deep breaths and her breasts lifted Pin's light body. Then gradually, almost reluctantly, she slid her feet toward her body until her knees were up. Pin's body then settled itself down, down between her thighs. She was pressing her pelvis up against him. I stroked her forehead and her hair. I touched her shoulders and her neck.

Her head moved faster and faster from side to side. Her mouth opened and closed as she gasped for more air, her tongue extending each time to touch Pin's face. I stroked the sides of her body and followed her smooth skin down to her thighs, gently squeezing as I went along. She was lifting her body up and down in slow rhythms now, pressing it harder and harder against Pin.

"He's cool, smooth. He's good and gentle. We're together and we're safe."

"Yes," she said. "Yes, yes." Her rhythm increased and became harder, rougher, more demanding. Pin's body bounced on hers. I had to place a hand on his back to keep him from falling over on me. She got wild, just the way she used to. Pin was ecstatic. I could see the excitement and satisfaction building in his face too. She moaned and twisted herself in a frantic effort to quiet the violent sex that had built up within her. "Yes," she said, "yes, oh yes."

"We're together. You, me and Pin. It's good." I didn't know if she could hear me, but I said it. She was kissing his face. She lifted her breasts so that the nipples turned into him. Her moans got louder and louder and more frequent. It went on and on and on until finally her body exhausted itself and began to slow down. Her hands dropped to her sides. She turned away from Pin and became quieter. I guided him off and she turned on her right side, facing the wall.

Without speaking, I dressed him again. Our work was done. Ursula had come back to us. As I lifted him into my arms and turned to leave the room, I heard her gentle sobbing. Both Pin and I smiled.

"It was a long time," he said as we went down the stairs, "but I think it was what she needed."

"No question. And she took to it. Everything in her wanted to take to it. She doesn't like being apart from us."

"You go back up and spend some time with her. Just stay by her side for a while."

"Right," I said and put him back in his room. "See you in the morning," I added and left him. I

felt great. When I got upstairs, Ursula was still sobbing softly, with her body turned to the wall.

"Hey," I said, sitting beside her. "Hey, come on, don't cry. It's all right now. Everything's fine, good again."

"NO, IT ISN'T," she shouted, turning on me. She looked ugly, her face contorted. "I DIDN'T WANT TO DO IT. YOU MADE ME. YOU AND THAT . . . AND HIM. YOU'VE GOT SOME HOLD OVER ME, SOME POWER. I DIDN'T WANT TO DO IT, I DIDN'T WANT TO DO IT," she repeated and pounded me on the chest. Then she cried harder.

"I know how you feel. I'm not mad. It's all right, really. It's all right," I added, touching her shoulder. She pulled away. "There's no reason to feel this way, no reason."

"Just leave me alone. LEAVE ME ALONE."

"All right," I said. "I will." I got up and walked out of the room, slamming the door behind me. I stood there for a moment and listened to her crying. "Damnit, damnit," I said. I thought about telling Pin how she was acting but decided that I didn't want to upset him just when he was feeling so satisfied and confident. I went down and poured myself a drink. A little later the phone rang. It was Stan. His mother was dead.

Ursula sounded distorted on the telephone. Her voice seemed hollow and she spoke with exaggerated slowness. If Stan weren't disturbed himself, he probably would have noticed it, or else he thought he had just awakened her. He kept apologizing for calling so late. In the context of what he was saying, his apology sounded ridiculous. In fact, I thought the

whole conversation was hilarious and I had to muffle some laughter from time to time.

"I didn't know anyone else to call," he said. "I just thought of you. I had to speak to someone. I'm sorry. My aunt is in no condition to talk."

"It's all right. Really, Stan, it's all right. I wasn't asleep anyway," she said. That made me laugh. What a front she was putting up for him. She couldn't stand any mention of death. I almost broke in on the conversation and said, "Who the hell are you bullshitting, Ursula? And while you're at it, tell him why you weren't asleep."

"Do you want to come over?"

"No," he said. "I'd better stay here. There'll be things to do in the morning too. I'll try to call you as soon as I can."

"OK."

"I'm really glad I could talk to you."

"Me too," she said. What slop, I thought. "Good night, Stan."

I heard them both hang up. Then I put all the lights out and sat on the couch, waiting. A few moments later, Ursula called for me. I didn't answer. She called and called. I heard her go check to see if I was in my room or in the bathroom. Then she called again. I didn't answer. She had told me to leave her alone. She stopped calling and went back to her own room. After a while, she came out and called again. This time she pleaded for me to answer. I came to the foot of the stairs. It was pitch-dark because I had switched off the light in the living room. She called again. I started up the stairs slowly.

"Leon, why don't you answer?"

"You told me to leave you alone."

"I'm sorry." She went to the switch for the hall lights.

"Don't. I want to stay in the dark. I feel like being in the dark." She didn't touch the switch, but I knew she couldn't stand talking to me this way.

"That was Stan on the phone. His mother died," she said, as if that was the reason she needed to have the lights on.

"Go to bed, Ursula," I said. I walked past her to my room. She took hold of my arm to stop me.

"Can't we talk a little first? Just stay with me for a little longer. Please."

"If you want to talk, you'll have to come into my room this time," I said, and I went into my room and crawled into my bed. A moment later, Ursula was standing beside me. I didn't say anything so she slipped under the covers.

"I don't know why death frightens me, Leon. It doesn't seem to frighten you much, does it?"

"No."

"You're more like the doctor than I am."

"I'm not at all like him."

"You've got some of his strengths."

"Maybe, but I'm not really like him. Pin always says I'm essentially a different person."

"If they have the funeral tomorrow, will you go with me?" I didn't respond. "Will you?"

"Maybe. If I'm in the mood."

"Please."

"You'll have Stan, won't you?"

"He'll have to be with his aunt. Please."

"OK," I said. "Anything, just so you'll go to sleep and let me get some rest too."

"That's my Leon, my good Leon," she said,

stroking my hair. It annoyed me and I made her stop it.

"Go to sleep now, Ursula."

"OK," she said in a very subdued voice. She got out of the bed and walked back to her room. I watched her and felt a little sorry for being so rough. She looked so pathetic and frightened. I waited until I heard her lay down in her bed and then I called out to her.

"Are you all right now?"

"Yes. Yes, I'm all right."

I turned over and looked up into the darkness. Pin was sleeping below in the darkness too, I thought. Lately I had been thinking more and more about his being alone down there. I was thinking that I might move his bed up into my room.

When I woke up in the morning, I saw that Ursula was already up and dressed. It took me a few moments to sift out my thoughts and fully wake up. I realized that today we would again confront death. I remembered when I was very little and I had seen this dog killed by a car. It had been left on the side of the road for a road crew to pick it up. Flies buzzed about its opened and sticky mouth. Its pale pink tongue looked frozen stuck to the side. That morning I asked Pin in the office if the doctor could bring the dog back to life.

"Couldn't he give him a 'jection?"

"Oh, no," Pin said. "Even the doctor can't do that."

"Could he do it if it happened to me?"

"Maybe," he said. "It depends on how seriously you were hurt."

I looked at the doctor, busy at his desk. If he could do these things, I thought, I wanted to be like him.

Chapter 13

I WENT TO THE FUNERAL WITH URSULA. IF I HADN'T, SHE would have been greatly disappointed. There were few people there because Stan's mother hadn't had the opportunity to make many friends. Most of the people were really his aunt's friends. At least, that's what he told us later on. There was a short service. The rabbi appeared almost bored, definitely indifferent to the whole affair, I thought. I was amazed that Ursula wanted to go out to the cemetery too, but I guess she felt she owed it to Stan. She squeezed my hand hard when they lowered the coffin. Before we left, Stan came over and told Ursula he would be at the house late.

"I've got to stay home with my aunt and greet people," he said, and he limped back to her. We

watched him and then we drove off. Ursula was very quiet all the way back to the village. Snow flurries began to fall. It had gotten much colder too. I was glad to get home. I couldn't stand winter weather. I never could. When they built the ski hill further up the road from us, I thought I might take up skiing, but I never really developed enough interest to try it. Winter was never a wonderland for me, even as a young kid. I guess that's why I spent so much time indoors with Pin.

Anyway, when we got home, Ursula went right into the living room and poured herself a drink. I watched her drink it down quickly and pour herself another. She hadn't even taken off her coat yet. I thought that was funny.

"Miss Spartacus should see you now."

"I don't run my life according to what Miss Spartacus thinks."

"My, my, so touchy," I said. I went upstairs to think about how I would rearrange my room if I did move Pin upstairs. I wasn't going to tell Ursula about it. I didn't want to get into an argument with her over it. I knew how she felt. She was especially feeling guilty about the night before. What I would do is simply start moving some of his stuff up gradually, so that she would get the idea. While she was making supper, I went into Pin's room and discussed it with him. He was quite pleased with the plan.

"I always wanted to return to that arrangement someday," he said, "but I never wanted to force my desires on you and Ursula."

"You should have said something. In any case it was definitely a big mistake to separate the three of us that way."

"Yes, I think so."

I asked him not to discuss it at dinner. He didn't care because he wanted to hear all about the funeral. I did all of the talking. It was obvious that Ursula couldn't stand the conversation. She ate quickly and made a lot of noise with the dishes and silverware. But I didn't let it discourage me. I figured that she had to learn that things were not always going to go her way. We watched some television after dinner and then Pin and I went into his room to figure out what things would have to be moved up. She was still out there watching television, so I took an armful of Pin's clothing and walked through the living room. I didn't say a word, but I watched her out of the corner of my eye. She was shocked. She was about to speak up, but stopped herself. A little after eleven, Stan arrived. I heard him come in. Pin and I were in his room, waiting. I went to the door and opened it slightly so we could hear their conversation.

"How's your aunt?" Ursula asked. He said she was all right and then they were both quiet for a few moments.

"I've been doing a lot of thinking all day. In fact, that's about all I've been doing."

"I can imagine."

"I've got to get hold of my life again, build something out of it."

"What are your plans?"

"I want to go back to school, maybe law school. I always had a secret desire for that."

"So you'll be leaving then?" she said. I couldn't wait for his answer myself. To be rid of him so easily—it was too much to hope for.

"Well, that's another thing I've been thinking about. You know I've grown quite fond of you,

Ursula. From the moment we talked in the library, well . . . I've always felt good in your company. It's not easy for me to relax anymore, but with you . . . I don't know, I feel kind of settled and at ease. Do you know what I mean?"

"I think so." Her voice was very soft and very low. I had to strain to hear her. Pin kept saying, "What'd she say, what'd she say?"

"And I have the impression that you care quite a bit for me. Correct me if I'm wrong."

"You're not wrong, Stan," she said. I opened the door a bit more.

"So I thought, well . . . it wouldn't be much of a life in the beginning. I'm still trying to reorient myself to my body, this leg, and I've got years of school ahead . . ."

"You're asking me to marry you, aren't you?"

"That's it. What'dya say?"

"I don't know what to say. I mean, it comes as a surprise at this particular time."

"You didn't plan to spend the rest of your life in that library, did you?"

"I've never really thought about it."

"Listen," he said, "I wouldn't feel so damn urgent about all this if it wasn't for your brother and his Pin and all that. I don't think it's healthy for you to go on this way. Frankly, I don't think you'll be all there if it continues."

I was ready to rush into the living room and attack him, kill him right there on the spot, but Pin held me back. I expected Ursula to tell him off now anyway. She had come back to us. She wouldn't want to have anything further to do with him. This relationship would end right then and there, I thought. I held my breath in anticipation. After she told him off, I was

prepared to walk in and throw him out, wooden leg and all. But she surprised me.

"I know. He's worse. He's planning on bringing Pin upstairs to sleep in his room."

"Upstairs? Ursula, you've got to take action now."

"I guess I've lived under the hope that he would grow out of it and I've just never faced the facts."

"That's exactly it. Now listen. As soon as my mourning period ends, I'll take you to see the right people and help make all the arrangements."

"OK," she said. I nearly screamed and pounded the walls. Instead, I closed the door and turned to Pin.

"It's no use," he said. "That guy will destroy whatever good work we do. We've got to destroy him."

"That's the only solution."

"She's actually considering marrying him."

"I don't think there's any doubt about it. It's just as we thought. He plans to marry her and then have some psychiatrist declare me sick. Then they'd get all of it, the whole estate—the investments, the property, all of it."

"It'll never happen."

"You bet your life it won't."

"Don't let Ursula know what we've heard," he said. He was planning already. What a guy. "And don't let her think you disapprove of the marriage, if she actually wants it, that is."

"OK."

Stan didn't stay long that night. After he left, Ursula went upstairs and went right to sleep. I left the door open a little between our rooms, but she

closed it. She got up the next morning and went to work without saying a word about her conversation with Stan.

"Maybe she just said those things to him, but didn't really mean it," I told Pin. It was a thought, a hope, but Pin didn't buy it.

"No. She's probably having a hard time figuring out how to break the news to you, that's all. Expect it any day at any time, and remember, don't have an angry reaction. We don't want them to suspect a thing."

"Right."

That night and every night during the week of mourning, she went over to sit with Stan. When she came home each night, she went right to bed. I knew she was afraid to come walking into my room because she was afraid I would have moved Pin in. We decided it would help prolong the tension if we didn't do it right away. Every day, though, I did move some more of his stuff upstairs. She didn't say anything to Pin or to me about her plans with Stan. We didn't prod or act especially interested. Finally, around the breakfast table on Saturday morning, she broke the news. She spoke very quickly, looking down at the table most of the time.

"Stan's asked me to marry him and I think it would be good. Good for him and good for me. I hope that you'll approve, Leon. I think you like him. You know he likes you. He wants to go to school and perhaps go into law. I hope that things will work out, because I believe I'll be very happy."

"Well, Pin, you were right," I said, smiling. "Pin had those suspicions for some time."

"Did he?" she said, half smiling.

"Yep. He said, 'Leon, those two are headed for serious things.' Those were your exact words, weren't they?"

"Pretty near."

"But what do you think, Leon?" she asked.

"If you're sure it's what you want."

"Oh, it is. Yes."

"Then, by all means, get married. When do you plan to do it?"

"In a couple of weeks. Do you really feel that way? Really?"

"Sure," I said, laughing. Pin was very proud of my performance. I could see it in his face. "It'll be lonely here for us without you, but we always knew you'd be going someday, didn't we, Pin?"

"Always."

"Oh, Leon. You make me feel so good. I was hoping you would feel this way."

"Why shouldn't I?" I looked at Pin. He was almost smiling. "Pass me the butter, please." She did, and she watched me smear my toast.

"Leon?"

"Yes."

"You ought to think about moving on too, getting away from here, away from this place, away from the memories."

"Why?"

"You just should, that's all. Think about it, will you?"

"I'm perfectly content here and so is Pin. This is a very comfortable house."

"But you don't meet people. Neither of us have been meeting enough people. If I hadn't met Stan when I did . . ."

"Don't you worry about it, Ursula. Just do what you want. We'll be all right, won't we, Pin?"

"We have been up to now."

"We sure have."

"Just think about it, will you, Leon?"

"OK, I'll think about it. So, are you officially engaged?"

"I guess so. I didn't want him to go and spend money on a ring. He hasn't very much money now."

"Well, you could buy your own. You've got a great deal of money, Ursula," I said, and I winked at Pin. Ursula had no idea just how much money she did have.

"No, I don't think that will go over too big with Stan. Maybe later on."

"Suit yourself. He certainly won't have to struggle through college."

"Yes," she said, but she looked away.

Stan and she went out to dinner that night. Pin and I were in the living room when he came to get her. She was upstairs, still getting dressed. I let him in and we sat on the couch. Pin was in his chair, glaring at him. I could tell it bothered him because he avoided looking at Pin the whole time. Even though it hurt to do it, I was cordial and pleasant.

"Well, brother," I said. He laughed, but it was a nervous laugh.

"She told you all the news then, huh?"

"Yep. She also said you want to go into law."

"I thought I'd give it a try."

"Interesting."

"You've had no ambitions that way, have you?"

"I once seriously considered becoming a mortician," I said, looking over to Pin and smiling.

"A mortician? Why?"

"I don't know. It looked like creative work to me once—taking a body that's passed into rigor mortis, pale with death, and restoring it to a semblance of what it once was. That's creative, don't you think?"

"I suppose in a way it is, but I think you'd have to be a special kind of a person to want to do it."

"No question."

"What about Pin?" he asked in a lower voice, as if he didn't want Pin to hear.

"What about him?"

"Does he, or did he, have any profession?"

"He's a retired physician," I said. I was going to say more, but Ursula appeared.

"Are you sure you won't join us, Leon?" she asked. "I asked Leon to come out with us."

"Sure, why not? How about it, Leon?"

"No. Thank you, but you two have a lot to discuss. I'm not in the mood to go out tonight. Go ahead, have fun," I said. "Besides, Pin and I are going to have a game of chess tonight, aren't we, Pin?"

"Yes," he said. He wouldn't say another word.

Ursula looked at Stan. He looked down and then looked up, pulling his lower lip under his upper lip. He pushed back the hair that had fallen over his forehead and then limped toward the doorway. Ursula stood staring at me.

"See you later then," she said.

"Maybe. I might go to sleep early."

"Good night," Stan called, and they left. I stood by the window and watched them get into his car. He had to hobble along carefully in front of our house. There was some ice there and I hadn't done a thing

to get rid of it. I stood looking out even after they pulled away. I turned around when Pin spoke.

"We've got to plan this out well," he said. "There's no way to do it and please Ursula at the same time."

"I don't care about pleasing Ursula, not anymore. She brought all this on herself."

"This is a whole new role for me," he went on, talking as though he were merely thinking aloud. "The doctor and I were expert in keeping people alive, not knocking them off."

"It's a new role for both of us."

"But it has to be done. I can see that now. It has to be done."

"How do you propose we go about it?" I pulled a chair alongside of him. His forehead wrinkled in thought, just the way my father's used to when he was considering a diagnosis. I waited patiently.

"We've got to get him alone here, at a time when Ursula is away."

"Yes. That shouldn't be hard." We both thought a little more.

"I've got it," he said. "You call him, maybe tomorrow, and tell him you want to discuss Ursula's finances. Tell him, since their marriage is a certainty now, you feel he should know about all that's in her name. Tell him Ursula doesn't fully understand the responsibilities and he'll have to help her, take over your job. He'll understand and believe that."

"Of course. Brilliant."

"Tell him Ursula would be embarrassed to have you discuss it in her presence and you don't want to hurt her feelings. He'll understand that too, and chances are, he won't tell her he's coming over."

"That's good. Unless he tells his aunt where he's going, no one will probably know."

"Exactly. Now our story will be that he never came here. You see, even if he does tell someone he's coming, that doesn't prove he actually arrived."

"But what about his car?" I stood up and paced a bit. "His car will be parked outside in front of the house." A few moments passed and then Pin thought of something.

"We'll get rid of it, even before we get rid of his body. Take it up to the ski hill and park it in their parking lot, then get a ride down with one of the out-of-towners. That way, there'll be no one available to testify that they drove you back."

"Hey, you know, you're not too bad for someone who isn't so expert."

"It's just like chess. You make a move in your mind and then counter it. Think of all the counters possible and then you can move safely."

"Just one more thing," I said. "How do you propose we go about the actual extermination?" He liked the use of that word. I could tell. For a moment we looked at each other, dumbfounded. Then the idea came. It came to me almost as fast as it came to him, but I let him take the credit.

"The Jerry Leshner affair," he said.

I snapped right to attention and smiled. Then I slapped my knee and stood up laughing. I walked across the room with my hand on my forehead. I turned around and looked at him and laughed. He was smiling that smile of self-contentment, so I continued to let him think he thought of it first.

"Jesus," I said, "and the doctor had the phony leg in his office for months afterward."

"Months."

"You'd think that alone would have brought it to mind—I mean, since they have that in common."

"Yes, you'd think it would have."

"OK," I said. "I've had a lot on my mind lately."

"You're excused," he said. "But don't let it happen again." And then he laughed. It had been a long time since I heard him laugh so hard. Both of us just sat there laughing for the longest time. I didn't mind being made the butt of Pin's jokes. Most of the time, that is.

Chapter 14

I HEARD STAN AND URSULA COME HOME THAT NIGHT. I listened to their low mumbling, Ursula's giggling and her moans of passion. I was awake throughout most of it, lying there looking up into the darkness, comforted by the thought that it would all soon end. I imagined that when they did laugh, they laughed at something that concerned Pin and me. It was Pin's and my conclusion now that Ursula wasn't to be hated and blamed as much as before. She was being victimized and influenced by a force much stronger than her. It was as if she had been attacked by some disease. You might reprimand her for being careless with her health, but your main concern was to be against the disease itself. Pin had referred to the entire plan of extermination as a form of treatment.

"It is as if we are removing an infection," he said. I liked the way he put it.

"Right, Doc," I said. We laughed about that too.

We all had breakfast together the next morning. Everyone was happy and polite. Even Pin cracked a few jokes at the table. This was, of course, part of our plan. There were to be no seeds of suspicion. We were dependent upon the element of surprise. I asked Ursula if she had informed Miss Spartacus of her intentions to get married and therefore leave the library.

"Miss Spartacus is sick. She hasn't been in for a few days. She has a bad case of influenza. I'm planning to tell her when she comes back to work. I don't want her to have any added worries now."

"Very considerate of you," I said.

"Stan is going to help me in the library today," she said, looking over at him. Pin gave me a quick, worried glance.

"All day?" I asked, trying not to sound very interested.

"Up until two o'clock. Then I have to do some errands for my aunt."

"I see. Well, I think I'm going to do a little shopping myself today. I need a few things."

"Oh?" Ursula said.

"Yes. I'm going to treat myself to a new pair of shoes. I need some underwear and socks too."

"Drop into the library if you have a chance," Ursula said. I looked at her. Never had I dropped into the library.

"It's too quiet over there for me."

"I know what you mean," Stan said smiling. "I get so I'm even whispering after I leave the place."

Stan drove Ursula to work. It was nine o'clock.

That didn't leave Pin and me much time to make preparations. I took a cold shower to stimulate me. I was actually singing, something I hadn't done for years. Pin was happier too. We were both very upbeat.

I put on one of my nicer shirts and pairs of slacks. I spent way more time than usual on my hair, after giving myself a closer than usual shave. My skin was almost as smooth as Pin's. When I finally stood before him, he registered his approval.

"Looking good, Leon, looking good."

"I feel good," I said, slapping my hands together. "And I'm anxious to get started."

I suppose there are those who will say that to use the Jerry Leshner affair as a model upon which to build our own method of extermination was needlessly complex and inefficient. I could understand such a reaction, but for us, the Leshner affair carried a certain medical truth to it. It had been part of our experience, so we knew it well. But, most of all, and this is something we readily admit to be wild rationalization, it made it all seem less like a murder and more like a treatment.

Jerry Leshner had diabetes and he was an alcoholic. Is there any combination more deadly? He was a handyman who passed himself off as a carpenter. He was really supposed to be very good at it, but he was said to be unreliable. As a child, I grew up knowing him as one of the village characters, a drunk who could often be seen staggering home, muttering to himself, giving little kids nickels, sleeping on the bench in front of the movies, urinating in the open behind parked cars or off a little behind a building. He was a short, stout man with a very round face

almost always covered with gray-black stubble. The kids always made up a lot of jokes about him. Although he wasn't married, he lived with a woman named Lillian Deutch. She worked as a chambermaid in the Dew Drop Inn, and she liked to drink just as much as Jerry. My father was treating Jerry for diabetes, but it got worse and worse until gangrene set in in the right leg. It had to be amputated. In those days Pin and I followed my father's cases closely, read his reports and asked him questions. My father was hoping I would develop an interest in medicine and be like him.

Anyway, Jerry Leshner was very careless about taking his insulin. He would often forget or be too drunk to take his shots. My father put him on Protamine Sinc insulin in order to help him cut down on the amount of shots needed per day. Of course, as time went by, the dosages had to be increased, especially because of his consumption of alcohol. He would forget to eat after taking his shots and have bad reactions. When his leg was amputated, he went on disability. Working had kept him sober some of the time. Now he spent more time drinking.

One day Lillian came home from work and found him dead on the kitchen floor. He had injected three times his dosage. She blamed it on my father, telling everyone that my father had prescribed the overdose. Of course, it was a matter that was easy to check. Leshner's treatments were kept on file. Those people who hated my father for one reason or another helped spread Lillian's accusations. A lot of people didn't like my father's objective, impersonal manner. They thought he was coldhearted and indifferent to human suffering. They said he didn't

treat people, he treated cases. My father knew that he had this reputation in some quarters, but he didn't give a damn. He was always of the belief that they needed him more than he needed them. I think a lot of people who came to his and my mother's funeral came to gloat. I know Lillian Deutch was there. She wore this stupid-looking wide-brimmed hat with all different colors of feathers sticking out of the top.

One afternoon my father told Pin and me why he thought Jerry overmedicated. I had been waiting in the lobby to go home with him. The last patient left. He was cleaning up in the office, so I went in and sat on the stool next to Pin. Miss Sansodome asked him a question about Jerry Leshner's file and he started to talk about him.

"That man simply panicked," he said. "Not that it really made much difference. The way he was going he was bound to expire soon anyway." My father preferred the word expire to the word die. "He had this terrible fear that every limb of his body would be amputated before his actual death. He saw himself as a basket case. I know just what was going through his mind."

He paused and sorted out some instruments. I didn't think he was going to talk about Leshner anymore, but Pin nodded and smiled. He knew my father's ways much better than I did. My father turned toward Pin and me and laughed.

"He thought that since insulin counteracted the sugar in the blood and kept him alive, all he would have to do is increase the insulin three-fold and thus insure that no gangrene would set in in any other part of his body. He went berserk. He probably gave

himself a shot every time he had the fear of losing another part of his body." My father laughed again and turned back to his instruments. My curiosity had been aroused.

"What kind of a death is it?"

"What's that?" Pin responded.

"What's it like to die from an overdose of insulin?"

"Very uncomfortable. First, perspiration and cold, clammy feelings, and then insulin shock, coma. We could have brought him out of it if anyone would have walked in and found him reasonably soon afterward, but he was there by himself all day."

"I don't see why anyone would want to blame it on the doctor," I said, but it was a lie. Even at that age, I knew why.

"It's all part of the job. You get used to it," Pin said, and that was the end of the discussion. Lillian Deutch tried her best to keep people from forgetting it, but it gradually faded into an obscure anecdote—the Jerry Leshner affair.

So when Pin brought it up, I naturally was very eager to use what we had learned from it: the misuse of insulin was a dangerous thing. I guess we could have chosen any of a dozen ways to kill Stan quickly, but none of them would have satisfied my and Pin's desire for revenge. Pin was looking forward to it very much. I didn't want to do anything to disappoint him. He was so proud of being the one to first bring up the Jerry Leshner affair. I had plenty of syringes available. Most of my father's things were kept safely in his bedroom. It was simply a matter of purchasing the insulin.

"I don't want you buying the stuff around here,"

Pin said. "That would create some suspicions, some interest. Take a ride down to Middletown. Go into one of those big discount drugstores. Don't buy it all in one store, either, if you feel the druggist thinks the amount strange. If anyone does ask you why you're buying so much at once, tell him you're a diabetic going on a vacation and you don't want to worry about your supply. I don't think anyone will ask, but have that story ready. It's always good to have a story ready. Remember, think of the counters for every move."

"Right. And we'll need the sack."

"Get that in one of those big department stores down there too. It's always good to buy things in stores like that. People don't remember people so easily. Everything's so matter-of-fact and indifferent. Now, you're sure you've got something to make him groggy?"

"We'll use Ursula's Librium. I'll give him two capsules at once. You know how it affects Ursula."

"As long as it makes him a little groggy so that there won't be much of a struggle. We don't want anything broken, no evidence of any conflict in here."

"I understand."

"Then we'll just sit and watch. Did I ever tell you about that time the kid was brought in to see your father, the one who swallowed the big marble and got it stuck in his throat?"

"I told *you* about it. It happened here. They brought him to the house."

"Oh, yeah. Jesus, that's right."

"You're getting senile, Pin, old boy. The kid was straining hard just to get a little air down into his fat lungs. Remember? He was a little fat kid from

Oken's bungalow colony. His eyes were bulging and he kept clawing at his own body."

"Ursula never saw that, did she?"

"No. She was out in the back. I told her about it and she got sick to her stomach, even threw up. My mother blamed it on me. She was mad because Ursula dirtied the bathroom wall."

"Yeah, I remember your telling me that. Your father turned the kid right over on his head and bounced him on the floor."

"His mother screamed. Scared the shit out of me, but the damn marble slipped out."

"Only your father would have the coolness to think of doing that. What a guy. He's going to be very proud of you after this."

"Yeah," I said. "I'd better get going."

I was in Middletown a little after ten. There were so many people out shopping, though, that it took me forty minutes to buy everything. It was a pain just to find places to park in the parking lots. I had to remember to buy my new shoes and underwear and socks so Ursula would believe I wasn't home all day. The guy in the shoe store just couldn't believe I would buy a pair of shoes without trying them on. What did I care how they fit? I wasn't going to wear them anyway. I simply pointed to a pair in the window and said, "Give me those in 8D." He brought them out and went to the seats. I stood at the counter. I had scooped up five pairs of socks and three packages of underwear.

"Don't you want to try them on?"

"No," I said. He stood there with his mouth open, so I added, "They're not for me. It's a gift."

Pin was very proud of me for remembering to buy the shoes and socks and underwear. He had com-

pletely forgotten about the stuff when I left. I told him he was getting hardening of the arteries and we had a good laugh over it.

"How do you know the sack's big enough?" he asked. I had anticipated the question.

"After I bought it, I went into the men's room, locked myself in a toilet booth and stepped into it. It's big enough."

"Good work, Leon. Good work. You're learning how to use your head well, boy."

"Thanks," I said. It was nearly twelve. "I'd better go out to the pond now and chop out that hole in the ice."

"You'd better. There probably won't be time later. We've got to do it all and dispose of that car before Ursula gets home."

"Right," I said, and I went out to the garage for the pick. While I was there, I figured I'd move the wheelbarrow to the back of the house.

My father had a great many nice tools. He very rarely used them, but he felt he had to have them around the place. What usually happened was that he'd start a job and then lose interest in it. After that he'd call in professionals to finish it. Most of the time it cost him more because he messed things up, but I guess it was worth it to him. He got some enjoyment in trying. He never felt incompetent or inadequate either. The gardeners and carpenters who came to repair and complete what he had started all made it a point to compliment him for the smallest achievement.

As I stood there in the garage looking over his stuff, I felt a great sense of weakness and fear come over me. If he was such an incompetent at manual

things, what made me think that I could be a success? It took me awhile to shrug the feeling off. Anyway, my biggest shock came a few minutes later. It frightened me because neither Pin nor I had anticipated it. If we had forgotten about something like this, surely we had forgotten something else. It had snowed. It had snowed on and off for the last few weeks. The yard behind the house was covered by at least six inches. Sure, once I got to the woods, it wouldn't matter much; but anyone looking out the back window would see my footsteps. And what good was the wheelbarrow? I'd have to drag and carry the sack. I broke out in a cold sweat. Panic came over me. Time was ticking away. Think, I told myself, think, think. I ran back inside and told Pin. He took it calmly and sat thinking.

"How could we forget?" I asked quickly. "I don't understand."

"Relax. Just relax. Be calm. We'll work it out."

"Maybe no one will notice the footsteps."

"We can't take that chance. Our plans have to be changed some."

"What do you mean? Put things off now?" He didn't answer. We both sat silently for a moment.

"We're not taking the body out right away."

"We're not?"

"No. We'll move him into my room for a while. No one goes in there. It'll be safe."

"For how long?"

"We're due for some snow this week, aren't we?"

"That's what we heard on the weather report."

"Good. We'll move him out then. The new snow will make your footsteps indistinguishable, if it doesn't cover them up entirely."

"OK," I said. I smiled to myself. I knew why Pin wanted it that way. He wasn't fooling me. He wanted to be able to go into his room and gloat. He was so taken up with revenge that he wanted to cherish every minute of it and make it last as long as he could.

Chapter 15

AT ONE-FIFTEEN I BROUGHT EVERYTHING DOWN AND set it out neatly on the counter in the kitchen. I had purchased two vials of U-80 crystalline insulin. This gave me eighty units per cc. Each vial contained ten cc. I therefore had a total of 1600 units of insulin to inject if I wanted to. There was a two-cc hypodermic syringe in my father's old bag, which meant I would have to inject him ten times to use the entire amount. I decided that I would limit the injections to five and see what resulted. I was looking forward to the injecting. My father had trained me in the use of a syringe. It was part of his attempt to interest me in the medical profession. Once, when Ursula had an inflamed throat, he let me in-

ject the penicillin. She said I did it real well. I really concentrated on what I was doing because I didn't want to hurt her. I was so afraid that I would because my hand shook.

There she was, sprawled over the examination table. Her skirt was up and her panties down to her knees. I stared at the pinkish color of her buttocks. My father held the syringe in the air, demonstrating again how I had to grasp it firmly with my thumb in front and the index and middle fingers behind.

"The fourth and fifth fingers are flexed so as not to interfere with the stroke of the injection," he said. "Remember, keep the axis of the syringe at an angle of forty-five degrees, like this."

"I really don't think I'm ready," I said, still staring at Ursula.

"Nonsense. There's nothing to it, Leon, and your sister very willingly agreed to let you use her as your first patient."

"It's all right, Leon," she said.

"I want a deliberate, quick stab. It is less painful," he said, and he held the needle out to me. I took it reluctantly. He gave me the alcohol and I sterilized a portion of her pink flesh. "Now concentrate," he said. I looked at his face. The intensely serious expression had a sobering effect on me. Then I turned and I did it, just like that. Ursula didn't make a sound. Instantly it was over. I stepped back, awed by my own accomplishment. He took the syringe from me and Ursula turned and sat up.

"Well done," he said. "Well done." It was one of the few times he gave me a compliment for anything.

After I brought all the materials down to the

kitchen, I went out to the living room and sat with Pin. We were both very nervous now and neither of us had much to say. I kept looking at the clock. Finally I couldn't sit any longer, so I went over to the desk and took out the books and papers. After all, we had to put up some kind of facade and lead him to believe I seriously wanted to go over Ursula's affairs.

"You've got to take it easy, Leon," Pin said. "You look nervous, fidgety. If he should see you like this, he'll wonder."

"I'll be all right. It's the damn waiting."

"Well, we did think you had to go out and chop that hole. There's where most of the extra time would have gone."

"I know, I know." I sat down again. Finally it was two-ten. "He must've gone home by now. It wouldn't be more than ten minutes from the library to his aunt's place."

"OK, call."

I got up slowly and walked to the phone. My hands were trembling as I dialed. I tried not to let Pin see it. We were in luck. Stan answered.

"This is Leon," I said. I told him what I wanted to do, and I told him that I had to call secretly because Ursula would have been too embarrassed otherwise. "She's very sensitive about all this. She even made me promise that I wouldn't discuss it with you until sometime after your marriage, but there are things that you just must know. Things you're going to have to take care of for her. She's really a baby when it comes to finances."

"I understand."

"So if you could drop over, just for an hour, now that she's at work."

"Sure. I'm coming into town anyway to get some things for my aunt."

"How is she?"

"All right. She's with her daughter today, but . . ."

"You mean," I said waving over at Pin, "your aunt's not at home now?"

"No, but I promised I'd pick up her list and get these things for her."

"This won't take long," I said, and we hung up. Pin couldn't believe in our good luck.

"No one will know he came here. No one. Leon, we've got it made."

The news did encourage me a great deal. I felt much less nervous and much more sure of myself and our plan. It would all go well. Twenty minutes later, Stan arrived. I let him in and we sat down in the living room by the desk. His eagerness to learn all about Ursula's finances confirmed my original suspicions. To sweeten our revenge, I built up her wealth, making the prize (the prize he would never win) that much more desirable. Pin saw what I was doing and smiled approvingly.

"My father made some very good investments with his money, and I've kept them up in Ursula's and my name. After you're married, you might not want to hold on to them, but if the past means anything, they're well worth it."

"Sure. I don't plan any radical new moves."

"This stock here," I said pointing to a page, "has gone up thirty points since my parents were killed. Ursula has five hundred shares."

"Five hundred shares? You mean, at two hundred and twelve dollars apiece?"

"Sure, Stan," I said, smiling. I threw a glance at

Pin. He was dying to laugh out loud, but he held it in. "But don't you know much about the stock market?"

"Not much, I'd have to confess. I never had the money to play around in it."

"Understandable. Now you will have it," I said. "With this year's interest, Ursula's savings are up to forty-four thousand."

"You're not trying to tell me that Ursula saved forty-four thousand dollars working in that library?"

"No, Stan. This is money from our parents. This is Ursula's share. Of course, by all rights, Ursula owns half of this property."

"Oh, I don't see what she would want with that. I mean, after all . . ."

"Nevertheless, half belongs to her. There are some bonds and a few real-estate ventures I want to show you. But first, how about a drink?"

"Sure. Scotch and water," he said. He couldn't take his eyes off the figures I had written on the paper before him. I went to make the drinks. Pin watched me carefully. It was very easy to slip in two capsules of Librium. I made him a relatively weak drink because I didn't want his blood sugar up that much. There was no sense in doing anything to hinder the effect of the insulin to come, I thought. Pin nodded approvingly.

"Thanks," Stan said, taking the drink. He continued to eye the paper on which I had written the figures.

"Here's to your good understanding of things. May you and Ursula turn the money into a comfortable fortune for both of you," I said. He liked the toast and took a long drink. I looked at Pin and winked.

"So there's some real estate to look after also, huh?"

"Oh, yes. A long time ago, my father bought into a parking lot in Queens. It's not far from the airports, and, consequently, it has proven to be a very valuable piece of property. Look here," I said, writing some figures on the pad as if I had to keep them secret. "This was our share from last year's profits."

"Wow! She doesn't have to work a day in her life, does she?"

"Ursula doesn't understand any of this," I said, shaking my head. "You're going to have to take care of all of it for her. Money is such a bother to Ursula. She can't even balance her checking account from month to month."

"Incredible," he said. He closed his eyes and then opened them.

"Want another drink?"

"No, this seems to be too much for me now. I really shouldn't have drunk on an empty stomach."

"An empty stomach?" I smiled at Pin. "Here, just read this," I said. "It's a stockholders' report on our shares of T. Dayton Enterprises." I handed him the papers and got up. He read the material slowly while I walked back and forth in the room. Gradually, he started having difficulty focusing in on the pages.

"I'm sorry," he said turning around, "but I find it difficult to concentrate on all this at the moment. Perhaps I should take some of it home with me and give it a lot more attention."

"By all means."

"I mean . . . I suddenly feel tired. Stupid, but I . . . feel kind of . . . weak too." He wiped his face with the palm of his hand.

"Sure. Feel free." I watched him actually struggle to stand.

"I'm a bit groggy. It's almost as if, as if . . ." he looked down at his empty glass.

"As if I put something in your drink?"

"Yes. You did . . . didn't . . . you?" He staggered around to face me. I took his left arm and pulled him forward. That brought his wooden leg in front of his left leg and he tripped over it. He hit the floor hard, landing on his left side and shoulder. "What the . . ." I watched him struggle to get to his feet. He pushed up with his arms, but I pushed down on him until he was flat on his stomach, his head resting on the rug. I knelt down beside him. He was breathing hard, fighting to remain conscious and understand what was happening to him.

"Ursula's got all kinds of jewels too," I whispered. Pin laughed out loud. "You're going to have all of it. And there are all sorts of valuable things in her deposit box."

"Why . . . are you . . ."

"Doing this? Simply so you and Ursula can have a fine life together," I said, and I laughed. Pin laughed too. Then I pulled the pants leg up on the right leg and unfastened the wooden part. "You won't be needing this anymore," I said. I walked over and put it on Pin's lap. He laughed again. We both watched Stan struggle to sit up.

"Time, Leon, time," Pin said.

"Right. Stan," I said, "from now on, we'll call you Jerry Leshner." Pin was hysterical. I went out to the kitchen and brought back the tray. Stan had difficulty focusing on all of it. He rubbed at his eyes and blinked. I stood by and watched as he took hold of the side of the easy chair and tried to pull himself up

on it. The chair turned over on him and he fell back. "Very weak and sickly," I said. Pin nodded.

"No question."

"I say, doctor, do you concur with my diagnosis?"

"One hundred percent."

"Diabetes?"

"Severe. Diabetic acidosis."

"Exactly. Shall we begin treatment?"

"Immediately. It may be too late," he said, laughing. Stan, fighting hard now for consciousness, stared up at me with glassy eyes. I filled the syringe and rolled up the pants on his right leg again until I reached his thigh. Then I did a remarkable thing. I sterilized the spot with alcohol. I didn't even think about it, or realize what I was doing at the time. Pin told me about it later on. We laughed over it. It seemed to take a long time to give him four injections. I felt sure that was enough. When I was finished, I sat back with Pin and watched.

"Get your father's manual," Pin said.

"Good idea." I ran out to the dining room, where some books were kept on shelves, and brought back the Merck Manual, eighth edition. I turned quickly to the chapter on "Hypoglycemia (Insulin Shock), Symptoms and Signs."

"Let's hear it," Pin said. Stan's reactions were already starting.

"At onset, symptoms include sweating, flushing or pallor, numbness, chillness, hunger, trembling, headache, dizziness, weakness, changes in the pulse rate . . ."

"Check it."

"Right," I said and got on my hands and knees. I took his pulse. "Rapid."

"Go on."

"Increases in blood pressure, cardiac palpitation . . ."

"Oh, get the old stethoscope," Pin said. He was really excited.

"Right," I said and ran into his room and brought it out. Then I got on my hands and knees again and opened Stan's shirt. He was sweating like crazy. The heart was palpitating, all right. "Check," I said.

"Go on."

"If the hypoglycemia is not relieved, signs of CNS involvement appear. There may be restlessness, incoordination, thick speech, emotional instability, negativism, disorientation . . . subsequently in severe cases by coma and even . . . death."

We watched. He was salivating madly now and moving like an epileptic. We waited. Pin had even forgotten that he still held Stan's wooden leg in his lap. The time went by slowly. The convulsions slowly ceased as he moved into a coma.

"It won't be long now," Pin said, "before he expires. You'd better carry him into my room and get rid of his car."

I hesitated for a moment before lifting him. Suddenly the sight of him there on the floor had a sobering effect on me. When I went to lift his body, his pants leg went shapeless below the right knee. It revolted me. I closed my eyes and stood up with him in my arms. I could smell the sweat on his body. His head turned in toward my chest. I tried turning it away, but it stayed there.

"Move quickly, Leon," Pin said. I struggled with the door for a moment, and then, using his body, pushed it open. When I got inside, I dropped his body on the bed. He was heavy and I knew it would be quite a strain to carry his body out back to the

pond. I took a blanket out of the closet and placed it over him. Then I went back out and brought Pin in. He wanted to sit in the chair by the bed and watch. "Pull the blanket off his face," he said.

"Are you sure?"

"Hurry up. Get that car out of here."

"Right," I said. I did as he wished and left the room, locking the door with my key. Then I went outside to Stan's car. I had forgotten to get the ignition key from him, so I had to go back inside, open the door to Pin's room and pull back the blanket. "I forgot the key," I said to the surprised Pin. I found the key in his shirt pocket. Then I went back out and drove the car up the hill to the ski lodge parking lot. It was crowded up there, being a good snow week. I put the car at the far end, inconspicuous, I thought. I expected it would be a long time before anyone noticed it. As I walked back from the parking lot, I threw the ignition key into the woods. I can't have any evidence on me, I thought.

Getting a ride back down the hill wasn't difficult. I must have looked underdressed because three young women in a car picked me up almost immediately and chastised me for coming out in such light dress. They asked me a lot of questions about myself, but I was deliberately evasive. About three houses before mine, I asked them to stop and let me out. I thought that was a brilliant piece of work. Pin would certainly be proud of my clever thinking. Even if they were somehow questioned about a hitchhiker, they would trace me back to the wrong house. I waited for their car to disappear and then I ran all the way home. It was nearly six o'clock.

When I got inside, I nearly had heart failure. Stan's wooden leg had slipped off Pin's lap when I

lifted him to take him into his room. In my excitement I forgot to pick it up. Ursula was due home any moment. She could have walked in and found the leg there on the floor. I quickly scooped it up, unlocked Pin's door, and threw it into a corner of the room.

"Everything go all right?" Pin asked. That's when I told him about my clever decision concerning where I got off. He was impressed.

"Is he . . . ?"

"Not yet. Just close the door and forget about him. It's done."

"Yes," I said. "It's done." Then I heard Ursula come in the front door, so I quickly closed and locked Pin's. I turned around and immediately panicked. I had completely forgotten about the syringe and empty insulin vial. Everything was still there on the tray on the floor.

Chapter 16

INCREDIBLY, URSULA DID NOT SEE THE STUFF ON THE
floor. She rushed into the house, stuck her head into
the living room and shouted hello. I was standing in
the middle of the living room, frozen to the spot.
Then she ran up the stairs, shouting about how she
had to get ready quickly to go out to dinner with
Stan. I exhaled relief and picked up the tray, taking
it out to the garbage pail in the kitchen. I placed it all
in a paper bag and shoved it down deep into the
other garbage. Then I sat down in the living room
for a few moments and tried to catch my breath. On
the other side of Pin's locked door, Stan was either
dead or dying. Upstairs, Ursula was rushing around
to get ready to go out to dinner with him. This struck
me funny and I couldn't help laughing aloud.

I got up and slowly walked up the stairs, subduing giggles as I went along. I went into my room and got undressed to take a shower. Ursula was already out and getting dressed. Everything I did, I did slowly, calmly, with a great sense of self-assurance. I felt as though I were God, in control of everything—how Ursula would be feeling after a while, and what her future would be like. It gave me a feeling of power and strength. I took a slow, warm shower, and then, after drying, I went back to my room and lay down to wait. A half hour passed. Finally I heard Ursula coming back up the stairs. Her steps were slow and heavy. I could see the expression on her face and I knew just how she was feeling. It gave me a terrific kick, a great sensation.

"What's the matter?" I said. She was standing in my doorway, leaning on the right side.

"Stan's over twenty minutes late and there's no answer at his aunt's."

"Maybe he's on his way over."

"This is the first time he's been late."

"So what. He's probably reached the point where he's beginning to take you for granted."

"Not Stan. He's not ever going to be like that."

"Sure."

"What'd you do all day?" she said, making an effort to put her disappointment and frustration out of her mind.

"A little shopping in the afternoon, like I told you."

"Oh, yes. Let's see your new shoes."

"Over there," I said pointing. She picked them up and examined them. "Like them?"

"They're very nice. Where'd you get them?"

"Middletown."

207

She put the shoes down and walked to the window. After standing there for a few moments and looking out, she turned and walked to my dresser and fiddled with my hairbrush. I watched her work her fingers nervously. Then she turned around.

"What could be keeping him?" She looked at my clock and then started to pace again. I watched her carefully.

"How was your day?"

"Not bad. Miss Spartacus is still very sick, though. She could hardly talk on the telephone."

"She should be careful. Old people can't afford to get the flu."

"She didn't even go to the doctor. She's one of those health nuts, you know, believes she can cure anything with vitamins or fasting."

"The doctor never believed in vitamin therapy much."

"I know. He never cared whether or not we took our supplements."

"Mother believed in us taking them."

"But he made fun of her." She paused and took a deep breath. "Jesus, he's really late now."

"Are you sure you got the right time?"

"Yes. I'll try calling his place again," she said. I watched her dial. It gave me a funny feeling to watch. It was like observing a character in a movie after you've already seen the first part and you know more than the character does. Wouldn't it be funny, I thought, if he answered. I laughed aloud, forgetting myself for a moment.

"What's the joke?"

"I just remembered something the doctor told mother about vitamins once," I said, thinking quickly.

"Where is he, damnit?"

"I don't know," I said, getting up and putting on my bathrobe. "I'm going down to throw a steak on. You want me to throw one on for you too?"

"No. We're going out."

"Suit yourself," I said and left her there, sitting on my bed.

She came down twenty minutes later. I had the table set and the vegetables cooking. I put out a plate for her too. I suppose I shouldn't have. It was really flaunting too much. She saw it, but she didn't say anything. Instead she went into the living room and sat on the couch. I watched her from the doorway. She waited a few minutes and then got up and paced. Then she sat on the couch again. I took out my steak. When I sat down at the table, I heard her dialing again. After she hung up, I called out to her.

"There's plenty here. Want to join me?"

"I really should," she said, coming in. "It would serve him right for being so damn late."

"Here," I said, cutting off a piece and scooping some vegetables onto her plate, "sit down and eat something. If he comes, you can go out for a drink or something. You've got to eat."

"I suppose you're right," she said, and she sat down with me just the way she used to before Stan had interrupted things.

"How is it?"

"I'm too mad to taste anything," she said but she ate. She looked up from the plate suddenly and looked around the room.

"What's the matter?"

"Isn't . . . where's Pin? Isn't he hungry tonight?"

"Oh, he ate earlier," I said, pleased that she was

concerned about him. Things were returning to normal quickly. I felt like the doctor looking at his recuperating patient. "He had skipped lunch. He's in his room, reading."

"Oh. Jesus," she said slapping her fork down on the plate. "You don't think something happened to him, do you?"

"There's no way of knowing for sure," I said, shrugging. "You tried his aunt's again?"

"No one answered."

"So he must be somewhere with her," I said. She liked that possibility and went back to eating again. "You want some coffee?" I asked after we both had finished.

"I'll make it. It'll help keep my mind off of him."

"Fine." I got up and went into the living room to watch the news. Things were just the way they used to be—Ursula was clearing the table, getting ready to make coffee, and I was sitting in the living room relaxing. Oh, Pin, I thought, how right you were. We did what was necessary.

Ursula and I had our coffee in the living room together. Time passed. It was eight, then nine, then nine-thirty. Every twenty minutes, Ursula called Stan's aunt's place. At ten o'clock, his aunt answered.

"No," Ursula said with great disappointment, "he's not here. I thought you'd know where he was. I see. Yes. I'll call you the moment he contacts me. Yes." She hung up and turned to me slowly. Her eyes were big. I did all I could to look serious and concerned. It was an incredible strain.

"What's the story?"

"She says he's not there. She just returned from her daughter's."

210

"Oh."

"When she came in, she found a note from him. All it said was he was coming over here." She brought her hand to her mouth and looked away for a moment. I didn't say anything, but what I thought was he probably wrote that note before he came over to see me. How lucky we were that he didn't write he was coming over to see me especially. "I think I should call the police," she added, turning back to me.

"Don't be stupid. Wouldn't that be embarrassing? Maybe he didn't want to come over here, Ursula. Maybe he got cold feet about you and the marriage."

"Never."

"OK, never, never. Meanwhile, if you go and call the police and they find him with someone else, what will you look like, huh?"

"Well, what can we do?"

"Nothing. Wait, that's all. You can call him in the morning."

"You expect me to go to sleep tonight, wondering?"

"What else can you do?" I shrugged and looked so innocent that if Pin were sitting out there with us, I'm sure he would have broken out in hysterics.

"Will you take me out for a ride, just so we can look around for his car, check a few places?"

"Oh, Ursula, come on, will you? Where would we look? And besides, suppose he tried to call you here and we were out?"

"I can't stand this waiting." She was close to tears. "I can't."

"Let's have a drink. It's good for the nerves at this point."

"I don't want one."

"Just a little drink," I said. "You'll feel better."
She didn't refuse again, so I made her a nice strong
highball. She sat drinking in the easy chair while I
watched television. We both had two more drinks
before I got up and shut off the set. "I'm tired."

"You go on up," she said. "I don't feel like
sleeping yet."

"You're being stupid."

"Please, Leon. Leave me alone. I couldn't sleep
even if I wanted to."

"Suit yourself," I said. I hesitated for a moment,
looking at Pin's door. It was safely locked. I was the
only one with the key, but the thought of her sitting
out there by herself, and him in there on Pin's bed,
was a thought that worried me. I don't know why.
Nevertheless, I wei   ostairs. I stopped by the
intercom and pressed the talk button.

"Pin. She's sitting outside of your room, waiting.
She won't come up. I suppose he's . . ."

"He's dead, Leon," I heard him say. His voice
was raspy, low, strained. "He has truly expired."

"Then tomorrow, maybe, we'll get him out to the
pond."

"It's all right. I don't mind. Go to sleep."

"Right," I said, and I went into my room.

A little while later, Ursula came up. I could hear
her sobbing. She went into her room and sprawled
out on her bed and continued to cry. I ignored her. I
knew what she was after now. She wanted my
sympathy and attention. It was her way. I let her go
on that way for the longest time. Then she grew
quiet. I waited. Sure enough, she started in again.
Finally, I got up and walked to the door to look in on
her.

Still dressed, she lay there curled up, clutching her pillow. It was pathetic, but all I could do was smile. It reminded me of the time I smashed in the face of one of her dolls and she had a tantrum that lasted an entire afternoon. My mother ignored her and my father was at the office. Finally, it was I who went in to calm her down. Naturally, I apologized and promised to get her a new doll. She was only eight years old at the time.

I walked over and put my hand right on the back of her exposed thigh. She turned over and looked up at me without saying anything. Her crying subsided. She wiped her face and took some deep breaths. I stood there looking down at her and waited.

"Now," I said slowly, "is there really any sense in your spending the whole night crying like this?"

"He didn't call. He just never came."

"So that's that."

"No," she said quickly. "I can't believe he would do such a thing. Leon, something's happened to him. We've got to call the police."

"We've been through all that, Ursula."

"Please," she said, sitting up and taking my hand. She pressed the back of it to her cheek. "Please, Leon."

"So do it," I said. I knew what she wanted.

"Won't you do it for me? Good Leon, you've always been my strength," she said, still caressing the back of my hand. She even kissed my fingers. It was too much. I had to turn away or I would have broken out laughing.

"Want me to look the fool, huh?"

"Please."

"OK, OK, I'll call. I can see I won't get any sleep around here until I do, anyway."

"Thank you, Leon. Thank you," she said. I pulled my hand away from her and walked out. First I thought I should perhaps confer with Pin before doing anything else. But then I figured there was really no need to bother him. I'd make the call just to hurry along the process of getting her to forget Stan. We figured the police would be called in at some time. The sooner we got that part over with, the better. As I walked down the stairs, I heard Ursula coming behind me.

"Maybe," she said from the top of the stairs, "maybe they know something already . . . an accident, maybe, or something . . ."

"We'll see." I picked up the receiver and dialed the operator, asking her to connect me with the police. After a brief moment, I heard a tired, very bored voice.

"Yes, this is the police," he said. Ursula stood in the living-room doorway, holding on to the wall.

"My sister had a date with her boyfriend tonight," I began. "He never showed and he never called. She's very worried about him and we figured we had better call."

The policeman sounded annoyed at times. His questions were very matter-of-fact in tone. I told Ursula he sounded like an answering service. I gave him a description of Stan (I emphasized his attractive physical qualities only because Ursula was standing right nearby), told him where he lived, his aunt's name, and for some reason, threw in the information about his mother's death.

"Was that a '70 or '71 Chevelle, Ursula?" I asked. I knew her ignorance of cars.

"I don't know." She bit her lower lip.

"I think it's a '71," I said. It was a '70, but I

214

figured telling him it was a '71 might delay the finding of the car even more.

"Ask him if there have been any accidents," Ursula prompted.

"Have there been any accidents involving cars or persons that fit that description?" He told me no and I shook my head at Ursula. She took a deep breath of relief. The policeman promised to get back to us and I finally hung up. "There's nothing more we can do now," I said, "except get some sleep." I didn't wait for her to say anything further. I walked past her and back upstairs to my room.

I expected that she would come into my room at this point. Ursula could never stand being alone when she was very afraid or very unhappy. Her dependence upon me at times like that has always filled me with pride. I suppose it has also aged me beyond my years. It has made me more of a father figure in some ways. I have always tried to provide for Ursula's needs; and I must say that up until her involvement with Stan, she was always very appreciative about it and eager to do what she could for me. When two people have such a good relationship, you really can't blame one of them for reacting violently when the relationship is threatened. Those were Pin's exact thoughts on the subject and those thoughts had a most profound influence on me.

I wasn't surprised to turn over and find Ursula standing beside my bed. She didn't speak. She just looked at me and then began to pace back and forth. I folded my arms behind my head and lay there watching her. There was something pathetic and yet humorous about it. I suppose I had a dumb smile on my face because when she turned around and looked at me, she seemed confused.

"Leon," she said, "I feel very frightened. I keep thinking the phone's going to ring and it's going to be the police to tell us of a terrible accident. It's going to be just like the phone call we got about mother and the doctor."

"You're talking yourself into something, Ursula."

"I can't help it. I can't think of anything else."

"You ought to try to get some sleep."

"I could never do it. I'm even afraid to close my eyes. All I'll see is Stan's body mangled in an auto wreck."

"What a gruesome imagination."

"I can't help it."

"Stop saying you can't help it, damnit." I sat up.

"I'm sorry." She stopped pacing and sat at the edge of my bed. She was staring across the room at some of Pin's things I had brought up. "Leon?"

"What?"

"Why would you want to crowd Pin in here with you when he has a room all to himself?"

"We've been through this before."

"I know," she said in her most ingratiating tone of voice, "but what I'm saying is true, isn't it?"

"I don't mind sharing my room. I don't need all this space."

"But just think of the effort—bringing him up, taking him down, bringing him up . . ."

"I don't mind the effort," I said and rubbed my lower legs. My body began taking on that creeping numbness again. It traveled up my legs, reaching my hips quickly. I had the craziest feeling, just as though I had stepped into ice water and I was going down deeper and deeper. I must have looked frightened too, because Ursula's expression changed immediately.

"What's wrong?"

"Just my legs fell asleep. It's nothing," I said, lying back.

"Maybe you should see a doctor, Leon. You've had that problem before."

"I'm just very tired, that's all. It's all right," I added sharply. "Let's go to sleep."

"OK," she said. She sounded very small and frightened. I really felt sorry for snapping at her. I took her hand and held it for an instant. She smiled, leaned down, and kissed me on the forehead. Then I turned toward the wall and rushed at sleep, desperate for the sanctuary within it.

Chapter 17

I AWOKE VERY SLOWLY THE NEXT MORNING AND HAD A great sense of confusion. My sleep had been an extraordinarily deep one, and coming out of it was more gradual than usual. After a moment or two, I remembered that Ursula had spent the night with me, but when I turned over, she was gone. I listened for her for a while because it was very silent in the house. That surprised me. I sat up, wiping my eyes and rubbing my cheeks to bring some sensation of life to my face. Then I looked out the window and clapped my hands in joy. It was snowing. It was a light snow, with tiny, tiny flakes, the kind of a snow that goes on for quite a while. Things couldn't have worked out better. I was eager to get up and get started. I listened for Ursula again, heard nothing,

and then got up and quickly slipped on my pants. Her clothes from the day before were still lying on the chair in the corner. I went to the bathroom and washed in warm water. The thought of cold water on my face made me uneasy for some reason that morning.

When I finished dressing and went downstairs, I found Ursula sitting at the kitchen table, staring at the clock on the wall. She had a cup of coffee before her but apparently had prepared nothing else. I stood there in the doorway, looking at her for a moment without speaking. She was dressed for work and her hair was combed back tightly and pinned behind her head. She was so still and neat looking that I was reminded of a manikin in a department store window. Apparently she had gotten up very early because it was only seven-thirty now.

"Is that all you're having for breakfast?" I asked, moving to get myself a cup of coffee too.

"I've been sitting here since seven staring at the clock. I haven't the nerve to call his aunt."

"Well, I'm glad to hear that. The poor old lady's probably fast asleep at this hour."

"I'm not afraid of waking her. I'm afraid of what she'll tell me. I don't want to hear her say that Stan's not there and hasn't been all night, or Stan's been in an accident," she said. She spoke in a dry monotone, stiff-necked, staring ahead. I felt she was really in a bad way.

"If he had returned, don't you think he would have called?"

"Yes, but I still have to call her."

"So call her." I took out some eggs and set up the poacher. "Want some eggs?"

"No, I'm not hungry."

"OK," I sang out and began making myself some breakfast. I got a tough day's work ahead of me, I thought, better have a good meal. Ursula got up and approached the phone. She stared down at it dramatically. I had to look away. I listened to her dial, slowly, carefully. I could hear the phone ringing and ringing. She had the receiver a little away from her ear. Then I heard Stan's aunt.

"Good morning," Ursula said. "I'm sorry if I woke you." That was all she said. Stan's aunt did the rest of the talking. Ursula listened and listened. Finally she said, "Thank you. Yes, I'll keep in touch."

I turned and looked at her quickly and then went back to the poacher. She went back to the table and sat down.

"OK," I said. "So what did she say?"

"What I expected. She called the police too. She called early this morning. There's been no trace of him. Leon, what do you suppose could possibly have happened to him?"

"I don't know. Anything. Maybe he just got tired of the whole scene—you, me, his aunt, his wooden leg—and split. Maybe this is an aftereffect of his war experience. I don't know. How should I know?"

"Well," she said, getting up reluctantly, "I guess I'll go to work and try to keep busy in the library. It might help me to keep some sanity today. If you should hear . . ."

"Don't even say it. The moment I heard, I would call you." She started out. "Ursula," I called as I set my eggs on the table, "you're going to have to face the possibility that he just pulled out."

"Maybe," she said. I was encouraged. At least she

was finally admitting to the possibility. "I'll call at lunchtime anyway," she added and left.

I had a great appetite. When I looked out the window, I saw that the snow had gotten harder and bigger. Things looked perfect. After I cleared the table, I went to Pin's door and unlocked it slowly. There he was, sitting vigil over Stan's lifeless body. The room was dark because the shades on the windows were drawn and the gray, overcast, snowy sky sent little light through them. Pin didn't even notice my entrance because he was so involved with Stan. I cleared my throat.

"Everything all right?" I asked.

"Perfect."

"You don't know how right you are. If you could just peek out that window there, you'd see a made-to-order snow."

"Really? That's great."

"I'll go get the sack. The earlier I do this, the better. More snow to cover my tracks."

"Right. You look sharp this morning. How's Ursula taking it?"

"As expected. She'll snap out of it with time. Already I've gotten her to admit to the possibility of his having run off."

"That's wonderful. OK, go to it," he said, and I went out to the garage to get the sack and pick. It wasn't too difficult to get Stan into the sack. All I had to do was slip it over his legs and then stand him up for a moment. His body dropped down like a cast-iron weight. I didn't look at him much because his face was so ghastly to me. But when I lifted him, I had the feeling I was lifting a thing instead of a man. For a moment I felt nauseated and dizzy. I had

to set the sack down and turn away. Pin didn't say anything. He knew what I was going through. After a few deep breaths, I was myself again.

"I'll take him out the back door."

"Of course. He's heavy. It'll be rough going. The pond's quite a distance."

"I know. Once I get through the open backyard, I'll drag him some."

"When you return, we'll have a drink together and celebrate."

"Right. Here I go," I said. I knelt down and grasped the sack around the middle. He was very heavy. With great strain, I lifted him onto my shoulder and straightened up. Then I reached out and took the pick. It was difficult to navigate myself through the door and past all the living-room furniture as I went through the house to get to the back door. A few times I banged into things, and once I nearly lost balance and fell over with him. By the time I had gotten out the back door, I was already puffing madly.

"Christ," I muttered to myself, "how the hell am I going to make it? I've got to make it," I answered. The snow was very heavy now and there was a strong wind that carried the flakes right into my face. My feet sunk about three inches into the hard crust that was there before, making each step a great effort.

The woods were about twenty-five yards behind the house. I had to stop and rest about midway. That was a mistake, though, because it took an even greater effort to lift him back up and over my shoulder once I started again. Also, the sack made a large impression in the snow. I had completely overlooked the fact that it would, and I chastised

myself for being so careless. I didn't tell Pin about that when I returned because I was totally ashamed of my own stupidity. As I stood there catching my breath, I stared at the old set of swings that had long since rusted. Ursula and I had spent little time on them. They're the kind of playground toy you enjoy more with friends around, and since we had so few friends, we hardly used them.

The snow was getting down the back of my coat collar. I had to tighten the neck button, but that made it harder to breathe. I was struggling for breath with Stan's body on my shoulder, so I unbuttoned it again and let the damn snow penetrate my clothing. The snow was falling so hard that I could barely see where I was going. Most of the time I walked with my eyes closed, taking big, ponderous steps. I used the pick to brace myself from time to time, and that also made an impression in the snow. I comforted myself by thinking that no one would ever figure out what all these impressions were anyway. Also, the way the snow was falling, it would all be nearly covered in a matter of hours.

I was grateful when I finally reached the woods. The cover of trees made the blinding snow less annoying. I stopped again, lowering the sack to the ground, this time confident that the woods would serve well to hide the traces. I stood there for a few moments, trying to catch my breath and prepare myself for the distance I had yet to cover. Looking around the woods, I was reminded of times when I was young and I used to come into the forest to be alone and imagine my own little world. I could still hear Ursula calling me afternoons, trying to get me to come out and play with her. I would stand behind a tree and peer out at her straining to be heard. Her

eyes closed and her face contorted under the great effort as she screamed my name over and over. Ursula always hated to play alone, no matter how many toys my parents bought her. She needed me to help her imagine and create.

I thought I saw a curtain move in a window facing the back of the house. It was probably Pin checking to see how far I had gone. I knelt down again and struggled to get the sack over my shoulder. When I stood up, I almost toppled backward and had to cling to the side of a tree for balance. Then I began to plod through the forest, following a pathway I knew well. I had to rest again before I reached the pond. And when I started once more, I forgot to take the pick and had to drop the sack and go back for it. I bawled myself out for my own carelessness and stupidity. I spoke aloud. In fact, I was talking aloud most of the time. I held a whole conversation with Stan in the sack.

"We're almost there," I told him. "You'll like the old pond. Ursula and I spent many afternoons there. I caught a fish there once, with just a hook and string and a piece of bread. I threw the fish back in because Ursula felt sorry for it. That's the way Ursula is, even today. She can't stand to see the smallest creature hurt.

"I want you to know," I went on, "that I have nothing personal against you. Pin and I both believe that, under different circumstances, we might have liked you a lot; but you must understand, we're doing this for Ursula, and you care for her too. Not as much as we do, I know."

Then I felt weak for having explained and justified my actions to a corpse, so I shut up for a while. I

plodded on and on. The steps grew more and more difficult and at one point along the way, I actually feared I wouldn't make it. I wondered if I would be able to just leave the sack in the forest and come back the next day and complete the job. But then I thought how much that would displease Pin, and there were the new footprints to consider.

"You've got to do it," I told myself. "You've got to and that's that."

Finally I reached the pond. It was completely frozen over, of course. I set the sack down nearby and walked out on the ice. It was much thicker than I expected. Nevertheless, it would be much easier to break an opening in the ice than dig a grave in the frozen earth. It was the best way. I began to chop. It took a great deal of effort and I had to stop many times to rest. The snow was coming down like mad now. I couldn't see much farther than the woods. After I broke through the section below me, I chipped away at it carefully. Gradually the opening grew larger and larger. I measured the diameter with the pick until I felt it was big enough to take the sack. Then I went back to the shore and dragged the sack out on the ice. These last few steps seemed to be the most difficult, despite the fact that I was pulling it over the ice.

When I got it to the hole, I felt along Stan's body. I figured I'd have an easier time of it if I could straighten him out some when I lifted him. So I grasped him around the waist and stood him up that way. At that point the damnedest thing happened. The strings came loose at the top of the sack and his head popped right out of it. I was standing there looking right into his face. It was almost as if he had

come back to life. All the while I treated him as more of a thing than a person, and now his head popped out to face me. I did a dumb thing then. I dropped him and he folded up, half in and half out of the sack. For a moment I grew very nauseous and dizzy. I had to go back to the land and sit on an old log to catch my breath. I looked out at him. A hand had come out and was resting on the ice, palm down. I made up my mind never to tell Pin about this part.

Slowly I got up and moved back out to the hole. I stuffed his body back into the sack and tied it very tight. Pin told me to twist the pick into the rope so that the weight of the tool would help sink and keep down the sack. The pond was at least eight feet deep so that was no problem about anyone finding him in the springtime. The water was usually dirty anyway. A kind of black humus ran in with the fresh water and gave it an inky appearance, although I imagined the water was good enough to drink.

"In a way I suppose I'm polluting," I said, "but it has to be done." I laughed and felt a little better. When the pick was secured, I lowered the sack into the opening. The water took to it immediately, making it a heavier and heavier weight. It sank slowly as I let it slip through my fingers. When I felt his head between my hands, I held it tightly for a moment and then I let go and the whole sack disappeared. I stood there looking down at the opening in the pond for a while and then I started back. I broke a branch and used it to cover over some of the footprints, just like I saw characters do in the movies.

When I got to the house, I looked back at the woods for a moment just to actually convince myself

it had all been done. Then I entered and took off my boots and coat. Pin was waiting anxiously for my report, but I didn't go right to him. I had to make a fire first and feel the warmth on my face and hands. His body had been so cold in that sack, and now it was freezing in the water. Pin heard me and called out.

"Coming," I said. I went to the cabinet and took out some rye. The whiskey warmed my stomach. I felt a lot better. "It all went smoothly," I said, going into his room. "Just as we planned. It's all done." I poured him a drink.

"Good," Pin said. "Now let's put it all out of our minds and go back to the way things were."

"I'll drink to that. Of course, it'll be a little while before Ursula . . . shit," I said, looking over in the corner.

"What's the matter?"

"That damn leg. We forgot all about it."

"No problem," he said, after a short pause. "You've got a fire going out there, haven't you?"

"Right."

"Just throw it right in."

"Good thinking," I said and picked up the leg. I brought it out, opened the grate, and threw it in over the logs. Just then, the phone rang. It was Ursula calling from the library.

"Has there been any call?"

"Nothing."

"Miss Spartacus came to work, but she doesn't look well at all. She's been coughing all morning."

"Damn stupid of her."

"I want to come home, but I hate to leave her."

"It's probably not too intelligent of you to be

around her anyway. I'm sure what she has is very contagious. You'll get it and then you'll give it to Pin and me."

"I can't stand the silence in here. All I do is think and think and think."

"Ursula, if you're fishing for me to tell you I want you home, I want you home. Does that help?"

She was quiet for a moment and then she said, "I'm going to tell her that I can't stay. Maybe she'll be smart and close the library for the rest of the day."

I told her to do it and hung up. A few minutes later, the phone rang again. It was Ursula with a new problem.

"What if Stan comes to the library to see me?"

"What if he does?" I said, imagining him swimming up to the hole in the ice, pulling himself out of the pond, shaking himself off like a dog, and walking downtown to meet Ursula.

"Well, I won't be here. I'll be home."

"So he'll call you at home, Ursula," I said in the same tone of voice I'd use if I were talking to a complete moron.

"No," she said. There was a recognizable note of determination in her voice. "It's better if I keep busy. At home I'd only drive you crazy and myself as well."

"Suit yourself," I said. This time I hung up before she could add another thing. I went back and told Pin all about her. "It's not going to be easy with her for a while."

"It's all right. We can deal with it."

I wanted to do some more work on my poem and sat down to do the writing. The words weren't coming easy. My mind kept drifting. Then, approxi-

mately twenty minutes later, the phone rang again. I was in a rage. If it was Ursula and she was going to go through her idiotic indecisions again, I was determined to hang up on her immediately. It was Ursula, but she had something entirely different to say; something quite disturbing.

Chapter 18

"SLOW DOWN," I SAID. "YOU'RE TALKING SO FAST I can't understand a word."

"It's Ralph Wilson. He stopped in to see me and they're going to drive me home. They want to speak to both of us."

"Why? What . . . I don't . . ."

"The car, the car. I just told you, Leon. Didn't you understand me?"

"How can I understand you when you babble into the phone and to someone else at the same time? What about what car?"

"Stanley's car. They found Stanley's car."

I put my hand over the earpiece of the receiver as if I could keep the words from coming out. Then I turned to Pin.

"She says they've found Stanley's car."

"How? When?" I gestured for him to be patient and put the phone to my ear again. Ursula was still trying to carry on two conversations. I shouted for her complete attention.

"Are you sure about that? How did they find his car?"

"We'll answer all the questions as soon as I get home, Leon."

"I don't understand. Why are they bringing you home now?"

"I told you. They have some questions. We'll be there in a few minutes," she added and hung up before I could ask anything else. I held the receiver for a moment and then hung up and told Pin.

"There's no reason for any panic. Their finding the car doesn't mean anything. Go throw some cold water on your face. You look flushed and they'll want to know why. Calm down, will you."

"Right, right," I said and did what he told me. I was sitting in the living room when Ursula and the police arrived. Along with Ralph Wilson was an old-timer, Pappy McGraw.

"How you been gettin' along, Leon? I just was tellin' your sister here how's I haven't seen you for some time now."

"Fine, fine, I've been getting along fine," I said. I made no attempt to invite them into the house. I thought we'd just talk in the corridor. Ursula took off her hat and coat quickly. I could see she was quite excited. "My sister says you found her boy-friend's car?"

Ralph Wilson spoke with an official voice. "As soon as you called, we checked with motor vehicles

and got his plate number and make of car. I handled it myself. It was a '70, not a '71."

"Everything's computerized these days."

"Sure the hell is," Pappy said.

"Where did they find the car?"

"Up in the ski hill parking lot."

"How did you find it?" I asked, swallowing hard. A sense of frustration and anger began building in me. It would be a damned efficient son of a bitch like Ralph Wilson who would find Stan's car so quickly.

"On my routine checkup," he said, not even a note of pride in his damned officious voice. "As soon as I got the make on the car, I started doing my rounds, checking the village and the surrounding area."

"But what made you think of going up there and checking the ski hill?" I tried to sound interested in his police skills.

"There's a restaurant and bar up there, a nice lounge too. Lots of people go there. There are rooms up there. It's a ski lodge, you know." I nodded.

"Then you found him?" I looked to Ursula. She was shaking her head.

"Oh, no," Ralph said. "He wasn't anywhere around. I checked the entire place. The automobile was locked and left in the lot."

"He could have been in one of the rooms, as you suggested," I said, avoiding Ursula's gaze.

"No, I checked. No one could even recall seeing him up there."

"Then . . . I don't understand."

"Well, neither do we," Pappy said.

"Your sister doesn't see any reason why Mr.

Friedman would go up to the ski hill, being he has a wooden leg and all," Ralph said. "Did he mention anything to you that might throw some light on it?"

I pretended to give it some thought, bit the inside of my left cheek and tilted my head.

"No, no, can't remember any mention of it. He might have just gone up there to look at the action. That's all I can think of."

"I see."

"Of course, he certainly could have met someone up there and traveled off with him or her. That would explain why he left the car there."

"It's a logical explanation," Pappy said, looking from me to Ursula. She looked hopeful but confused. There was a moment of silence during which I felt Ralph was studying me.

"Yes, it's logical," he finally said, "but there are other possibilities."

"What do you mean?" Ursula said quickly.

"No sense in guessing," Ralph said. "Now, you're sure there weren't any arguments, not between you and Mr. Friedman and not between Leon and Mr. Friedman?"

Ursula looked at me.

"Nothing that I know of, no."

"Well, we've got a good description of him from you and from his aunt," Ralph said.

"This sure is a big house," Pappy said. It was a statement purely from left field, but I welcomed it.

"We don't use all of it."

"Just the two of you," Pappy said nodding at the walls. Ursula shot a terrified glance at me. I could see she didn't want any mention of Pin at this point.

237

"That's why we don't use all of it," I said, smiling. Ursula breathed relief.

"OK," Ralph said, reaching for the door behind him. "We'll be in touch."

"Please," Ursula said. "The moment you know anything, anything at all."

They both said good-bye and left. The moment the door closed, Ursula's expression changed. She looked like a small child again. "Now I'm really worried," she said.

"Now I'm not," I replied and started for the kitchen.

"What do you mean?"

"Oh, c'mon, Ursula. It's pretty obvious, isn't it? He left his car up there and went off with someone. Probably a girl he met at the lounge."

"I don't believe it."

"You mean, you don't want to believe it. There's a difference." She followed me into the kitchen. "Let's have some tea and relax. Once you get a chance to think this thing out intelligently, you'll see I'm right."

"But what do you suppose Ralph Wilson meant by 'other possibilities'?"

"Nothing. He was just being dramatic and overly important. Don't you remember him in high school? He was always one of those hall monitors, ready to turn someone in for cutting into line or pushing. I never liked him."

"Still, it makes me shiver," she said, embracing herself.

"The tea will warm you up. Go into the living room and sit by the fire I made. I'll bring it in."

"I think Mrs. Spartacus closed the library once

she saw I was really going home and she'd be alone.
. . . She looks terrible. I was afraid she'd die right
there."

"I can't think of a better place for a librarian to
pass away, can you?"

"Oh, Leon, you've got such a dry sense of humor,
just like the doctor had."

She went into the living room. I thought about the
snow filling up my footprints in the backyard, and I
smiled at the clever way I had handled my return
from the pond. I had taken great pains to step in my
own footprints, thus making it look as though
someone had gone into the woods but had not
returned. Later, when Pin and I could sit and relax
alone, I planned to tell him all about it. He enjoyed
those kinds of details. He had given me a plan, but it
had only been in a sort of outline form. I had filled it
in, and at the moment, I was very proud of my work.

Somehow, I thought, this is all going to find itself
in my epic poem.

"Pin's in his room," I called. I knew she'd be
wondering about him. "I'm going to put some rum
in your tea. That's sure to make you feel better.
Then I'll get Pin and the three of us will relax
together. Just like old times, eh?"

"Whatever you think, Leon," she said in a very
tired voice. "I don't feel like doing a thing."

"There's nothing for you to do. I'll have you
warmed up in a little while," I said. I started to
whistle. I remember having this feeling of elation,
this tremendous surge of optimism. I was tapping the
teakettle lightly with a spoon, getting her cup and
saucer ready, dancing and swaying as I took down
the bottle of rum from the cabinet over the sink. In

my mind things weren't going to just be as they were before, they were going to be better than they had been before.

"How are you doing?" I shouted out to the living room. There was a moment of silence. Then she answered, straining for volume.

"OK, but your fire's just about died out."

"I'll be right in there to build it up," I sang out. The thought was just beginning to fight its way out from some dark passage of my mind and broke out into my consciousness when Ursula replied.

"It's all right. I'll do it. I need to do something," she said. I had the kettle still in my right hand and I froze in position. There was no scream. My heart was pounding. I was about to relax, believing it had burned up in the fire. Then I heard the crash of china, some of the knick-knacks on the mantel above the fireplace. That was followed by silence. I turned and waited. More silence. Carefully, I put the kettle down on the stove and turned to the doorway. When I stepped out into the living room, Ursula was standing there looking down at the wooden portion of Stan's leg in her hands. It was charred some, but otherwise pretty much intact. Perhaps it had been treated with something to prevent it from burning. Perhaps the fire hadn't taken to it. I don't know, but there it was.

I'll never forget the look on Ursula's face at that moment. She looked up at me with an expression of such awe and horror that even I was suddenly taken with the grotesqueness of what had occurred. Her mouth opened as if she were voicing a great scream. The skin of her face pulled back, twisted, wrinkled. Her eyes squirmed, closed and opened with slow movements. It was as if she were trying to focus in

on something. She looked down at the leg again and then dropped it at her feet. I wondered if it had been very hot to the touch. She backed away, staring down at it, all the while not making a sound. I took a few steps forward and looked down at the leg as if I were seeing it for the first time myself.

"Where's Stan?" she said, her voice high-pitched, straining. All I did was shake my head. "What have you done?" There was such a mixture of fear and pity in her. I had never seen anything like it. I actually stepped back, shaking my head. I wanted to feel as outraged as she was. I couldn't stand being on the defensive. The first idea that came to my mind was, it wasn't my fault.

"I don't know," I said. "Pin. Pin must know," I added. I even nodded my head for emphasis, just the way I used to when Ursula was a little girl. "Pin will tell us," I heard my little boy's voice say. "Pin knows everything, Ursula."

Did she scream? I really can't remember. I know it sounds stupid, but there were so many thoughts going through my mind at the time and I heard so many voices screaming at me from the past. My mother was shouting about her rug being messed up by the ashes of the charred leg. My father was losing his patience over my poor interest in a medical profession. Ursula was having a temper tantrum because I just sat and stared at her silently, pretending to be Pin. All these memories rushed down on me at once. So you see, it's not so unreasonable for me to have forgotten whether or not she screamed.

She ran out of the room and up the stairs, pulling on her own hair as she rushed by me. I remembered that. Then the whistle on the teakettle began. Those details are clear. I walked back into the kitchen and

turned off the stove. My hand was shaking. I stood there for a long time thinking, going back over every detail of the afternoon. All my care and caution, all my cleverness destroyed by one dumb action. It really wasn't all my fault either. It was his. He had made the suggestion. He should have known better.

"You," I said, busting into his room and pointing at him seated in his chair. "You who always considers the counters, the obstacles, the difficulties first; it's your fault."

"What's my fault?"

"The leg. You told me to throw it in the fireplace. You told me to do it."

"So?"

"She found it. It was your idea. YOUR IDEA!" I screamed. He smiled at me. The conceited, pedantic bastard smiled at me.

"Calm down, Leon. This is no way for a rational man to act. Think of your father, of his coolness, his sureness in times of great crisis."

"Screw his coolness, damn his rational mind. Ursula found the leg. She knows."

"Everything?"

"Not everything, but she knows."

"You should have checked to be sure the thing had burned up."

"She knows!" I shouted. He didn't answer. He wasn't going to deal with me when I was in such a state. I could see that on his face. "Damn you," I said and left, slamming the door behind me.

I approached the stairs gingerly, trying to understand what had gone wrong with such a perfect plan. Everything had seemed so well done. I looked back at Pin's closed door. On the floor of the living room, the charred leg remained, defiant, confident, a part

of him that had lingered to destroy us. I rushed back and picked it up, slapping it many times against the stone of the fireplace. It chipped some, but it didn't crack.

"Damn you," I shouted again, and I threw the leg at Pin's door. It left a mark, a black ash spot. "Damn you," I muttered under my breath, and I walked back to the stairs. I looked up. They suddenly appeared very steep and very difficult to ascend. I began to go up, taking each step slowly, my eyes fixed ahead at the doorway to Ursula's room.

Chapter 19

SHE WAS SITTING IN THE DARK. I LOOKED AT HER, SEATED there on the bed, her hands in her lap, staring out at me. I couldn't see her face, but I could see her rigid posture. I spent a few moments standing there, waiting to see what she would say. I had no plan in my own mind, no idea how I would start or what my angle was going to be. I kept thinking, however, that I was now in this terrible spot because Pin had told me to throw the leg into the fireplace.

"Now listen," I began, stepping into the room. "I know how this thing looks to you. I can just imagine what's going through your mind," I added, and I laughed. It was a very artificial laugh, and I regretted it immediately. "But there is really no reason for you to act this way." She didn't say anything. I

246

reached over and switched on a small lamp in the corner.

Slowly, I walked further into the room until I was standing very near her. I wanted to look at her face. Although I was a little to the right, she continued to stare straight ahead. She blinked every few seconds, but that was the only movement visible. Her hands remained clasped in her lap. I deliberately brushed up against her right shoulder. She didn't turn and she didn't say anything.

"Are you just going to sit there without speaking?" I waited. All she did was blink. "You're acting ridiculous, sulking like a little girl." She didn't speak. I walked away and stood by the door, looking out at the stairs. "OK," I said, turning around, "so Stan was here. I didn't want to tell you about it, because of what happened between him and Pin." I waited, figuring she had to show some interest now, but she didn't respond. All she did was continue to sit there, staring out, rigid and silent.

"They had an argument, you see. It all happened while I was away," I went on, walking back toward her. "Remember, I went shopping . . . the shoes and stuff?" I was going to sit down beside her, but quickly changed my mind. "No use hiding the truth any longer. Pin never liked Stan. No matter what I said, he found fault with him. He didn't trust him from the start. You know how Pin is. When he forms an opinion about someone, he's stubborn and insistent. That's the way it was with him and Stan. I talked myself silly nights trying to get him to take another point of view. Honest I did, Ursula." I waited. There was no response. "Damn it, Ursula. Are you just going to sit there without speaking forever?"

I walked back to the door quickly, turned, and then went directly to our adjoining door. I went into my room, put on the lights, and flopped on the bed. I could wait, I thought. I could wait for her to be reasonable. Meanwhile, I thought about the details of what had supposedly happened between Pin and Stan. I was sure she would want to know. I waited and waited, but she never did call to me. It was very unnerving. I assumed she had gone to sleep. At least an hour or so must have passed before I got up and looked in on her again. Would you believe it? She was still sitting there in the same position, staring at the doorway. It really got to me. I became a little nervous; maybe even a little frightened.

"All right," I said, walking into the room. "This has gone far enough." I went over to her and shook her, but she didn't change her expression, nor did she look at me.

"So you want to know about it, so I'll tell you," I said. I paced about for a few moments. "When I got home from shopping, Stan was sprawled out across the living-room floor. He had been drinking before he came here. Pin said he started right in on him. He said Pin was ruining our lives; living off us like some sort of a parasite. Pin said he was very uncouth, violent. He wanted Pin to move right out, claiming that you were reluctant to marry him because you were afraid to leave me here alone with Pin. Did you ever hear of anything so ridiculous? Pin argued, of course. He's never been one to stand by and permit himself to be abused by anyone. The argument got worse, heated. Stan actually became violent. He was very drunk by this time, having taken some liquor out of our cabinets too. Pin said they wrestled about for a few moments. Fortunately for him, Stan was

too drunk to be effective. He fell backward and hit his head on the fireplace stone."

I paused to see if she would respond now; perhaps ask questions. But she continued to stare ahead, blinking. I paced about a bit more, wondering if it did any good for me to go on. I planned to go down and tell Pin the story I had concocted just in case Ursula questioned him. He'd go along. He had to, since he had been the cause of her finding things out.

"When I came home, I found him sprawled out, as I said," I continued, turning back to her. "Naturally, I was very disturbed. It was a great shock. Pin told me what had happened. He was very upset. Even though it really wasn't his fault, I knew that if we reported it to the police, there would be investigations and many embarrassing questions. So I drove Stan's car up to the ski lodge and . . . and I disposed of his body. When I lifted him off the floor to carry him out of the house, his leg came off, probably due to the struggle with Pin. It was Pin's idea to throw it in the fire," I said quickly. "I never would have done it if I hadn't been so distraught. He thought it was the best way." I waited. She still did not respond.

"You can understand why I had to get rid of his body, can't you, Ursula? I'm sorry you had to find out the way you did. I was planning on telling you in time, quietly. So you see, there's really no sense in your continuing to behave like this. I think . . ."

I stopped talking because I could see tears had come out of Ursula's eyes. They were traveling with jerky motions over her cheeks and dripping off the sides of her face and the bottom of her chin. However, she didn't change her position or stop blinking.

"Poor Ursula," I said sitting beside her. I put my

arm around her, but she didn't lay her head on my shoulder like she always did. I patted her arm and stood up. "I can understand how you feel, but after you get over the immediate shock, you'll realize that things wouldn't have worked out anyway. Not if he behaved the way he did with Pin. We still have each other. We'll be all right," I said. I was beginning to hate the sound of my own voice. She still hadn't said a word. "Want me to get you anything?" I asked. "You could indicate a yes or a no," I said sharply, but she acted as though she hadn't heard a word I had said.

I stomped out of the room and went downstairs. Hadn't I been patient with her? Hadn't I made an unusual effort? Sure, she was disturbed. She had been through a great deal, but I had only tried to help her. She could have shown some response, some gratitude, but she hadn't. I wasn't going to wait around for her to do me the honor of uttering a word. Instead I poured myself a drink and rebuilt the fire. I didn't invite Pin out either. Alone, I passed a few hours, thinking and drinking. At one point I got up, took the flashlight out of the hall closet and went to the back door. I opened it and searched the new snow to see if my footprints were gone. From what I could tell, they were. At least that part went well, I thought, and started back upstairs again. I had calmed down somewhat.

She was still sitting there on the bed, staring. I walked over and brushed some hair off her forehead. She blinked. Then I thought I noticed a slight rocking motion in her upper body. It grew stronger and stronger. It struck me funny, but I didn't laugh aloud. She looked like she was sitting on a horse-drawn wagon or in a car going over a bumpy road. I

placed my hand on her right shoulder and she stopped rocking.

"Jesus, if you could see how you look," I said. "You'd feel utterly ridiculous." Naturally, there was no response. "It's getting late now, Ursula. You should go to sleep. You're emotionally exhausted." All she did was blink.

Ursula was wearing a button-down sweater and a skirt. I knelt down and slipped off her shoes. She was wearing panty hose. Slowly I unbuttoned her sweater. She sat like a baby, limply. I worked the garments off her body carefully. She offered no resistance, but she offered no cooperation either. After I unfastened and removed her bra, I tried to get her to lie back so I could slip off her skirt and panty hose, but she wouldn't move out of the sitting position. I didn't want to force her back. Looking down at the whiteness of her breasts, I was taken with the quietness of her body now. There wasn't so much as a slight quivering. I leaned over and looked into her face. She blinked. An artery on her neck pulsated as her heart forced blood around her body. I touched it with my fingers just to feel the beat of her life. She felt strangely cold and dry.

"You want to go to sleep, don't you, Ursula?" I waited but there was no indication that she had even heard me. I couldn't stand being ignored that way. My father used to do it all the time, but he was supposedly always in deep thought about one patient or another. I would just give up talking to him and walk away.

I continued to try to get her attention. "Ursula, Ursula," I whispered. She seemed to hear nothing. There was an emptiness in her eyes. She had the look of a blind person. I touched her bottom lip,

pushing it away from the upper one. Her teeth were clenched together within. When I withdrew my finger, her lips snapped back, sealing her mouth once more.

"You're being very stubborn," I said. "Very immature." Then I stepped away, because she was actually frightening me. "I'm just going to leave you here. Just like this, damnit," I added. I waited for a moment, and then I turned and went into my room. I got undressed and went to bed. When my eyes got used to the darkness, I looked out through the opened door. Vaguely I could see her still sitting there in the rigid position. "Damnit," I whispered, and I turned to face the wall.

I fell into a deep and restless sleep. Sometime during the night I awoke because I thought I heard a kind of muffled rapping or tapping sound. I lay there with my eyes opened, staring into the darkness, listening, but I could hear nothing. I concluded that it was just part of my present nervous state and I turned over again to force myself into what I believed was much needed sleep. I was still very tense and I remembered how my father used to say that mental anxiety was more exhausting than physical exertion. My mind was a veritable montage of surrealistic images. I saw Pin's body with Ursula's face. I saw Ursula with Stan's leg. I saw my father down under the ice looking up at me angrily. I know I must have tossed and turned most of the night because I wasn't rested. Just before early morning I had a final dream. I know it was just before morning because when I woke, the sun was just beginning to invade the darkness.

I dreamt that Ursula got up from the bed and, half naked, walked out the back door of the house.

Without shoes, she trudged through the new snow, sinking almost as far down as her knees at times, and made her way through the woods. She walked in a trance, pulled by some great magnetic force that kept her from feeling the intense cold. Snowflakes melted on her breasts. Little streaks of water, like thick tears, wrote cold lines all over her exposed body. When she got to the pond, she stopped and looked out toward the opening I had made in the ice. Gradually, she focused on it. She saw Stan's head bobbing in the water. His eyes were frozen closed. She saw it and then she began to scream and scream and scream, bringing her hands up to her ears to shut out the horrible screech of her own voice. That's when I woke up and sat up quickly.

It took a moment for me to realize it had only been a dream. I rubbed my eyes and then remembered how I had left Ursula. I studied the darkness between us. There was just enough light now to give me a vague visual awareness. She wasn't there.

My heart began to beat faster. A wild fear shot through me. My dream, could it be real? Was she out there in the snow? I panicked like an idiot, and I ran to my parents' room to get a view of the backyard. I stood there struggling to see through the thinning darkness, searching the snow for signs of fresh footprints. Then, still not realizing how ridiculous I was, I ran downstairs, got the flashlight again, and went directly to the back door. I opened it, and, standing there in my underwear, I faced the bitter cold and searched the snow for signs of Ursula. I guess the cold air brought me to my senses, and I shut the door and turned off the flashlight. Where was she?

I stood there for a moment trying to gather my

thoughts and get better control of myself. There was something trying to force its way up into my consciousness. It was something that had happened during the night. But my mind was confused by all the nightmare images that had passed through it. I couldn't think straight. I went over to the sink to wash my face in the cold water. Just as I dried it with a dish towel, I heard her shrill, piercing scream.

Chapter 20

FOR A FEW MOMENTS, I COULDN'T LOCATE HIM IN THE room. Ursula, still half naked, was sitting on his bed, her hands clutching at her ears as if to close out all sound. Her eyes were big and her face looked distorted—her mouth twisted to one side, her teeth pressing down on her lower lip.

My eyes moved to the ax on the floor. Then I looked up slowly to where I had left Pin sitting. I wanted to speak, to utter some sound, but my jaw wouldn't move. I moved in closer to look.

The ax had sliced clear through his upper torso. There were parts of him scattered all around the room. The right arm remained dangling from a part of the shoulder. There was no left arm, but the arteries and the tendons hung ripped from the stub.

The right leg had been severed at the knee. The left leg was apparently untouched. The head and neck were shattered all over. I saw an eye looking up at me from the foot of the chair. Parts of his teeth and gums lay by the wall to the right.

I tried to step back, but I couldn't move. The numbness that I had known in spasms all these years came rushing over me. I sank into the same ice water in which I had deposited Stanley's body. Ursula was looking at me, but the expression on her face began to change from a look of distortion to a look of amazement. In a moment, though, she was only in my peripheral vision, because I couldn't move my eyes. I was able only to look straight ahead.

I heard Ursula move forward on the bed until she was directly in my vision. Then she stood up and brushed her hair away from her face. Her face was streaked by dried streams of tears. She rubbed at them and licked at her lips until the dryness disappeared from them.

"Leon?" she said, but I didn't respond. I didn't even attempt to respond. I thought she was looking at me when she said, "Leon," but I couldn't understand why.

She turned and looked at the destruction around her and then back at me. I hoped she didn't expect me to put him back together again. I laughed to myself, although I couldn't feel my face move with the laugh. She was always like that—coming to me after she broke things. "Mend my doll. Fix my baby's hand."

Destructive, destructive. "You know there are things a doctor can't fix," I'd say. "Even me."

I wasn't about to play these dumb fantasy games and put a doll's broken arm in a cast. She'd have to

face reality. The sooner that happened, the better it would be for her. Sure I'm cold; sure I'm hard, but it's for the best. It takes strength to be this way, strength. The world is divided up into two parts: success and failure. Success comes to those who face reality head-on. It's as simple as that.

Now Ursula kicked broken parts of him away from her feet. She looked back at me with what I thought was a smile. Why was she smiling? What's so funny about destruction? She took hold of the front of his pants and pulled him right out of the wheelchair. Then she flung him into the far corner of the room. More pieces separated. She brushed the chair off.

"Each of us has killed someone we love, haven't we, Leon?" she said with such bitterness.

"Leon?"

"Oh, you're not going to talk; you're not going to move. You're going to be Pin? Is that your way of punishing me for what I've done to you? What have you done to me? WHAT HAVE YOU DONE TO ME?" she screamed.

I couldn't recall seeing her in such a state ever before. She was obviously in need of a tranquilizer or some sedation. I began to consider what I would prescribe. As a rule I'm not very fond of prescribing mood-control pills. I would rather see people work out their problems consciously. I believe pills are only a temporary solution. They don't get at the causes, only the symptoms. However, Ursula was acting so unusual. . . .

She rushed to the closet and pulled out a shirt and a tweed suit. She handled everything roughly and frantically. I wanted to tell her that the tweed could use some pressing, but in the state she was in I didn't think she'd care. She went to the dresser drawer and

took out a pair of knee-high socks and then went back to the closet to get a pair of black shoes. At least they had been recently polished, I thought.

"Oh, we'll play your game, we'll play your game," she said. She was chanting more than talking. "You're the one who couldn't face death. You're the one who was weak, who created ways to avoid reality. You, not me. OK, OK, don't let Pin die; don't let the doctor die. Let Leon die. LET HIM," she screamed. I felt so sorry for her. She came very close to my face. I could see the tiny red veins in her eyes. "I want him to die," she said slowly, pronouncing each word with separate and distinct emphasis.

She took the shirt off the hanger and began putting it on me. It was still nicely starched and clean. I welcomed the feel of it. She pulled it around roughly, though, and buttoned it quickly. I wanted to complain about that, but I figured she was just too disturbed to appreciate what I would say.

She went back to the closet and picked out a tie. I didn't care all that much for her choice, but as with the shirt, I kept it to myself. As she tied the tie, I saw the smile on her face spreading. Her eyes were dancing with light. She had the gleefulness of a little girl. Every once in a while she would laugh. Yet tears were coming from the sides of her eyes. She'd wipe them away and laugh and smile and work diligently on the knot of the tie until she had it perfect. At least she adhered to that. I always demanded perfect tie knots.

Then she smoothed the front of my shirt down against my chest and stepped back to consider me.

"Oh, yes," she said. She took the pants off the bed, and she moved me to the spot. I was happy to sit down. It took awhile for her to work the pants up

my legs. Afterward, she stood me up, grunting, struggling, but still uttering a small laugh here and there. She buckled my pants and put on the suit jacket. When I was all dressed, socks, shoes and all, she stood back and admired me, nodding her head, still breathing heavily from the effort. I thought I might say something about one of my cuffs, but I didn't want to do any damage to her self-satisfaction.

"And now," she said, "we'll put you where you belong, won't we?"

She brought the wheelchair forward and backed me into it. Then she wheeled me out to the living room.

"Now just let me get dressed and then we'll have tea, won't we? We'll have tea, tea." Her breasts quivered as she said the word. "Don't go away," she added and laughed again.

I was feeling so sorry for her. Such a state of mind, such a state. I sat there reviewing some similar cases I had known. I wondered what had put her in such a state. You can never tell what it is with women, I thought. Small things can do it almost as much as big things sometimes.

Something, though, something . . . I couldn't help feeling it was something terrible. I think I should try to find out, I thought. Before trying to treat her in any way.

I wondered. Could it have anything to do with that horrible mess in the bedroom?

EPILOGUE

THE LIVING ROOM WAS LIT ONLY BY THE LAMP ON THE table beside the easy chair. Ursula sat in the chair and held a book on her lap. She wore a white cotton blouse with a scoop neck and ruffled collar, a light-blue skirt, and a pair of high-heeled sandals. A charm bracelet dangled from her left wrist. Her hair, washed and brushed, lay in a smooth sheen over her neck and shoulders.

The rest of the room was subdued, the walls silhouetted with the distorted shadows of the furniture. He sat in the corner, in Pin's corner, barely illuminated by the fringe of Ursula's reading lamp. The weak light made his eyes seem deeper, hollow-like, glassy. The bony features of his face were skeletonized. His lips, firmly closed, were like a

seam sewn tightly. His arms rested on the arms of the wheelchair and his hands dangled at the ends, hung in afterthought, lifeless, frozen.

In fact, all of him seemed cut in ice, preserved. His eyes were rigid; he did not blink. Only on close inspection could one discern the slight, almost imperceptible movement his breathing created in his chest. His hair had been brushed and sprayed until not a strand was out of place.

It was snowing in heavy, wet flakes, the kind that stuck to the window and turned quickly into raindrops that moved willy-nilly down the panes, creating spider webs on the glass. Because of the angle of the lamplight, the rest of the outside world was cloaked in a curtain of black. Indeed, it seemed as though the windows hung on a wall of night. Only a counter light was on in the kitchen and the hall light that illuminated the entranceway and stairway.

The house was quiet. The wind moved over the shingles to make an undulating hissing sound. Occasionally one of the shutters on the side of the house would bang, but it had no rhythm or regularity.

Ursula smiled and stroked the cover of her book lovingly. It was wrapped in a thin, aged leather, and the imprint on it was almost rubbed out. It said, "Ursula's Book." She opened it gently, as though it would crumble in her fingertips.

"I know," she said, without looking toward the corner, "it's time. You want me to begin. Mustn't be impatient," she added in mock chastisement. "We mustn't rush, ever. Rushing only causes accidents. Yes.

"Shh," she said. "I won't begin until it's perfectly quiet. You must pay complete attention."

She paused. The angelic smile stayed with her.

She looked up from the book and into her own memory for a moment. What she saw and what she heard pleased her.

"It's my turn. I go," she said and lifted the opened book from her lap until she held it close enough before her to begin.

"*The Adventures of Pinocchio,*" she began. "Once upon a time . . ."

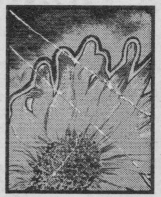
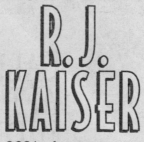

New York Times Bestselling Author

TESS GERRITSEN

A ringing phone in the middle of the night shakes newlywed Sarah Fontaine awake. Expecting her husband's call from London, she hears instead an unfamiliar voice. Nick O'Hara, from the U.S. State Department, is calling with devastating news: Sarah's new husband died in a hotel fire…in Berlin. Convinced her husband is still alive, Sarah forces a confrontation with Nick that finds them on a desperate search, trying to stay one heartbeat ahead of a dangerous killer.…

Gerritsen delivers "thrillers from beginning to end."
—*Portland Press Herald*

Available July 2001 wherever paperbacks are sold!

CALL AFTER MIDNIGHT

A hand grabbed my wrist and stumbled, catching a glimpse of Ashlee's shocked face as I fell into Steven. Bones ground beneath the pressure of his fingers. Steven's dark blue eyes blazed down into mine. His voice roared in the stunned silence of the room. "You're not listening to me." The scent of alcohol and mints blasted my face.

Slowly, distinctly, I said, "Ashlee, call security, please."

Steven blanched, the unhealthy red vanishing into deathly white. I caught his eyes and held them; caught myself as he moved, stepped back, releasing me. Covering my wrist with the fingers of my other hand, I massaged the sore flesh and bones. Oddly enough, my smile was still in place.

"Cancel that order, Ashlee," I said softly. "Steven, if you ever so much as touch me again, I'll file assault charges on you. If you ever curse me again, I'll take it to the hospital staff and board with a formal complaint. If you ever raise your voice to me again in an unprofessional manner, I'll do the same. You have something to say to me, say it in private. Understand?"

Steven nodded. Slowly he pulled his eyes from mine and stared at his hand as if it had gone berserk and grabbed me of its own will.

"And, Steven, please try to remember that you don't pay me here. I'm under contract to the hospital, not you personally." Even more softly I added, "I'm sorry I was late. Go home to Marisa. She…" My throat closed up and tears threatened again, the second time in two days. "She needs you." The last two words were little more than whispers.

Steven looked from his hand to me, his eyes strangely hollow and bewildered. "I—I'm sorry, Rhea."

My smile slipped. I wondered if that was what he'd said to Dora Lynn, the X-ray tech he had hit. I wondered if that was what he said to Marisa each time a drop of spinal fluid dripped from her nose, untreated. *I'm sorry.* "Go home, Steven," I managed to say. "Go home."